THE
UNEXPECTED
HONEYMOON

THE UNEXPECTED HONEYMOON

BY

BARBARA WALLACE

First published in Great Britain 2014
by Mills & Boon, an imprint of Harlequin (UK) Limited,
Large Print edition 2015
Eton House, 18-24 Paradise Road,
Richmond, Surrey, TW9 1SR

© 2014 Barbara Wallace

ISBN: 978-0-263-25601-7

Harlequin (UK) Limited's policy is to use papers that are natural, renewable and recyclable products and made from wood grown in sustainable forests. The logging and manufacturing processes conform to the legal environmental regulations of the country of origin.

Printed and bound in Great Britain
by CPI Antony Rowe, Chippenham, Wiltshire

To my fellow writers,
Donna Alward, Wendy S. Marcus,
Julia Broadbooks, Abbi Wilder and
Jennifer Probst, without whom I could never
have gotten this book written. Thank you for
showing up every morning and pushing me to
be productive. You ladies are the absolute best!

And, as always—Pete and Andrew,
you're my heroes!

CHAPTER ONE

"BUENOS DIAS!"

Having grown up in the hospitality industry, Carlos Garcia Chavez thought he'd seen everything. But nothing prepared him for the blonde standing in the doorway of the Presidential Villa. With her tight white dress and messy halo of platinum blond hair, she looked like she'd stepped out of a black-and-white newsreel. So much so, he half expected to hear her call him Mr. President in a husky stage whisper.

What he got was a big, overly bright smile that sent awareness shooting through him. Something else he was unprepared for. He adjusted his grip on the wine bottle cradled in his arm and pushed the unexpected reaction aside.

"Buenas tardes, Señorita Boyd."

"Oh, right, you say *tardes* in the afternoon.

My bad. I'm still on East Coast time. I'll catch on eventually."

Carlos refrained from pointing out that East Coast time would place her later in the day, not earlier. After all, the guest was always right, no matter how wrong they might be.

Meanwhile, this particular guest leaned. She leaned a hip against the door frame, a position that drew further attention to her curves. "So what can I do for you, Señor…?"

"Chavez. Carlos Chavez. I'm the general manager here at La Joya del Mayan."

"Did you say *general manager?* Damn. I knew this was too good to be true."

"There is a problem?" he asked. Carlos tensed. Errors were the kiss of death in the hotel industry. Mistakes led to bad reviews. He had enough on his plate keeping La Joya's current woes under wraps; he did not need to add to his troubles.

"Lucky for you, I haven't unpacked yet." He followed, trying not to stare at the way her bottom marked her steps like a white silk pendulum. "I mean, Delilah and Chloe might be generous, but seriously, this? Doesn't matter if they are married to millionaires. Well, Del's married to one. Chloe and her boyfriend aren't married yet, although anyone with two eyes in their head can see they're going to be. They're absolutely crazy about each other. Do you want some champagne?" She lifted a bottle from the coffee table.

"No, thank you." Judging from her rambling friendliness, she'd had enough for both of them. "You said there'd been an error?"

"I've never had Cristal before. This stuff is really good."

"I'm glad you approve."

"Oh, I do." She took a long drink, nearly emptying the glass. "I definitely do. I should have served it at tomorrow's night—I mean tomorrow night's reception."

"We can upgrade the menu if you'd like."

She snorted, for some reason finding his suggestions amusing. "Little late for that."

"Not at all. We can make changes right up to the last minute. So long as you're happy."

"Because everyone knows, it's the bride who matters, right?" A shock of blond curls flopped over one eye. She swiped them away with a sloppy wave of her hand. "Long live the bride."

Her groom was going to have his hands full tonight. Come to think of it, where was her groom? According to their records, Señorita Boyd booked one of their famed wedding packages, but the front desk said she'd checked in alone. Most guests arrived either as couples or with a gaggle of family and friends.

Only unhappy brides drank alone.

Stop it. The señorita's drinking arrangements were none of his business. For all he knew, she wanted to be alone. Her accommodations, however were his concern, and so he repeated his original question. "Is there a problem with your room?"

"Only that I'm here. That's why you're here, isn't it? To tell me I have to move?"

So that was her worry. His shoulders relaxed. "Not at all."

"Seriously?"

"I handled the upgrade personally." In fact, her friend, Señora Cartwright's, phone call had been one of the few positive highlights of his first week. "For the next week, consider this villa your home away from home."

"Really? Wow. I have the best friends." She looked down at her glass, her eyes growing so damp that for a moment, Carlos feared she might cry.

"If I recall, Señora Cartwright said you'd admired the photos in our brochure," he said.

The comment did its job, and distracted her. "More like drooled. This place is amazing. More than amazing, actually."

"I'm glad you approve."

"Oh, I do." Draining her glass, she reached for the bottle again. "So, Señor… What did you say your name was again?"

"Carlos Chavez."

"Car-rrr-los Cha-a-a-vez. I like how it flows off my tongue." She gave a tipsy grin. "You sure you don't want anything to drink?"

"Positive."

"Then why are you carrying a bottle?"

The Cabernet. In all the distraction, he'd almost forgotten the point of his visit. "My desk manager told me you talked with the Steinbergs while waiting to check in."

She drew her brows into a sensuous-looking pout. "Who?"

"The couple from Massachusetts who were staying at the Paradiso."

"Oh, right, Jake and Bridget. They'd walked up here from the beach. I told them they were wasting their time getting married at the Paradiso. I researched every destination wedding location in the eastern hemisphere, and none come close to being as romantic as this place."

Given his family's outrageous investment in creating said romance, Carlos certainly hoped so. The Chavez family prided itself on owning the most exotic, most enticing resorts in Mexico. "Apparently your enthusiasm was contagious because they placed a deposit for next spring."

"I'm not surprised."

She paused to wipe champagne from her upper lip with a flick of her tongue that left Carlos gripping the bottle a little tighter. He didn't know whether she always moved with such sensuality or if the alcohol unleashed some hidden sexuality gene, but he found himself reacting in a most unwanted way.

"They said they stopped by on a whim, but no one hikes four miles along a beach on a whim. Besides, Bridget had that look, you know? After five minutes, I knew she'd made up her mind. Can you believe the front desk wanted to send her away with nothing more than a brochure?"

Yes, Carlos could. "Unfortunately, we are between wedding coordinators at the moment," he told her. No need to explain the disaster he'd been sent to fix. "Thankfully, you were there to speak on our behalf. I wanted to come by and personally thank you for assistance, and to give you this with our compliments." He presented the bottle. "Cabernet from Mexico's own Parras Valley."

"How sweet. Mexican wine." She reached to take the bottle from him, only to stumble off balance and fall against his chest. Champagne sloshed over the rim onto his shirt, but Carlos barely noticed as he was far more focused on the hand pressed against his chest.

"I like how you pronounce *Mexico.*" There it

was, the husky whisper. Carlos's body stirred instinctively.

"Perhaps you and your fiancé can toast to a long life together."

Gripping her shoulders, he righted the señorita and thrust the bottle into her grip. A bit rougher than necessary, perhaps, but he wasn't in the mood to play substitute. The force caused her to stumble backward, although thankfully, she managed to catch her balance without assistance. Giving a soft "whoops," she smiled and swayed her way to the writing desk. "Nice thought, Señor Carlos. Unfortunately, he's off having a long life with someone else, and I don't feel like toasting that."

"Pardon?" She had booked a wedding package, hadn't she?

"My fiancé—ex-fiancé—decided he'd rather marry someone else."

No wonder she was drinking. He felt a stab of sympathy. "I'm sorry for…" Did one call a broken engagement a loss? No matter, he hated the phrase. *Loss* was such an empty and meaningless word. Having your world implode was far more than a loss.

"You're here alone, then," he said, changing the subject.

"Honeymoon for one." She raised her glass only to frown at the empty contents. "Wow, this stuff goes down way too easily."

"Perhaps you ought to…"

Blue eyes glared at him. "Ought to what?"

"Nothing." Wasn't his place to monitor her behavior. She was a guest. His job was to make her happy.

"Do you know what he said? He said I cared more about getting married than I did him. Can you believe it?"

"I'm sorry." What else could he say?

"Yeah, me, too." She swayed her way back to the coffee table. "Like it's a crime to be excited about getting married. News flash: It's your wedding day. The one time in your life when you get to be special."

Hard to believe a woman who looked like her needed a specific day to feel special, but then as he knew all too well, there existed women who needed constant reassurance, despite their beauty. Perhaps the señorita was one of those women.

"Besides, if Tom was that upset, why didn't he say something sooner? He could have said, 'Larissa, I don't want a fancy wedding,' but *nooo,* he let me spend fifteen months of planning while he was busy having deep 'conversations' with another woman, and then tells me I'm wedding obsessed.

"Seriously, what's so great about having deep conversations anyway? Just because I don't go around spouting my feelings to anyone who will listen, doesn't mean I don't have them. I'll have you know I have lots of deep thoughts."

"I'm sure you do."

"Tons. More than Tom would ever know." Turning so abruptly, the champagne yet again splashed over the rim of her glass, she marched toward the balcony.

He should go, thought Carlos. Leave her to wallow in peace. But he didn't. Instead, something compelled him to follow her outside to where she stood looking at the Velas Jungle, her shoulders slumped in defeat.

"I would have listened to him, you know," she said, the energy depleted from her voice.

"I'm sure you would have."

He joined her at the rail. It was the view that made La Joya famous. Across the way, snowy egrets had taken up their nightly residence in the mangroves, their noisy calls reverberating across the lagoon. The water rippled and lapped at the tree roots, creating a blurry mirror for the green and blue above.

The champagne glass dangled from her fingertips. He was debating reaching for the glass to keep her from dropping it into the water when she asked abruptly, "Are you married, Señor Carlos?"

The word *yes* sprang to his tongue, same as it always did. "Not anymore."

"Divorced?"

"Widower."

"Oh." Downcast lashes cast shadows on her cheek. "I'm sorry."

Again with the meaningless words. "It happened several years ago," he replied.

"My problems must seem really silly to you."

Her remark surprised him. Normally, people relaxed when they heard his answer, assuming the passage of time meant less pain and mistaking his numbness for healing grief. To hear her express sympathy, left him off balance. "I'm sure they don't seem superficial to you."

"But they are," she said with a sigh. "They're silly. I'm silly."

She was sliding into self-flagellation, dangerous territory when combined with alcohol. Old warning bells rang in his head. "Why don't we step back inside?" Away from the railing. "I'll get you a glass of water."

"I don't want water," she said, but she did push herself away from the rail. "I want more champagne."

As long as it moved her off the terrace. He stepped back, expecting her to turn around, only to have her cup his cheek. Her blue eyes locked with his and stilled him in his tracks. "I'm sorry for your loss," she said with far more sincerity than the word merited. Behind the kindness, Carlos recognized other emotions in her eyes. Need. Loneliness.

A spark passed through him, a flash of awareness that he was alone with a beautiful, vulnerable woman looking for reassurance. The similarities between now and the past were far too many, forming a dangerous rabbit hole down which he swore he'd never go again.

"Our staff is here for anything you need," he told her, breaking contact before other, more disturbing memories could rise to the surface. When it doubt, turn to business. The rule served him well these past five years. "We'll do our best to ensure you enjoy your stay, regardless of the circumstances."

"You're sweet."

On the contrary, he put an end to sweet a half decade ago.

After leading her inside, he made sure to lock the balcony door. With luck, she would curl up on the sofa and fall asleep. To be on the safe side, however, he made a mental note to have security keep an eye on the villa.

Images of a lifeless body floating atop water flashed before his eyes, stopping his heart.

Housekeeping, too. You could never be too careful.

The sun still beat strong on the sandstone walkway when he stepped outside. The beach side of the resort always remained sunny long after the lagoon settled in for the night. Guests enjoyed what they considered two sunsets. They would gather on their balconies or their private docks, margaritas in hand, and watch the shadows spread across the lagoon. A short while later, they'd turn their attention westward in time to see the sun slip behind the ocean. One more of the many perks that came with vacationing in paradise.

Personally, Carlos liked this time of day because the resort was quiet. Gave him time to walk the perimeter and ferret out any potential problems. There were always problems. Creating paradise took work—more work than people would ever realize. He'd been here six weeks now, not yet long enough to know all the resort's idiosyncrasies. Much of his time, thus far, had been consumed by cleaning up his predecessor's mess. Misused funds, unpaid accounts.... His predecessor's managerial incompetence knew no bounds. And of course, there was Maria. Stupid woman was supposed to plan weddings, not run off with the philandering idiot. A decade's worth of reputation in jeopardy because of two people's recklessness.

Rashness led to nothing but disaster.

"Whoops, excuse us." A pair of newlyweds cut around him to duck under the southwest archway, their arms filled with beach bags and each other. Carlos stepped aside, heaviness tugging at his heart as he watched the young woman playfully swat her husband's hand from her bottom. He'd been that way once himself, romantic and naive, believing the magic would last forever. Before a pair of needy brown eyes sucked him dry.

He wasn't an idiot. He was well aware there was more behind his family sending him to La Joya than righting managerial mistakes. They hoped that his tenure at La Joya might lighten his heart. As if being surrounded by romance would be enough to revive the man he used to be. What his family failed to realize was that man died. Destroyed by his own romantic

illusions and desires, he could never be resur-
rected again, no matter what his surroundings.

No, Carlos's days of romance were over. Best
he could do was let others enjoy the illusion while
it lasted. Or, in the case of Señorita Boyd, help
reality sting a little bit less.

Who turned on the lights?

Even with her eyes closed, the brightness
stabbed at Larissa's right eye. If she could cover
her face, maybe she could eke out an hour or two
more of sleep. She reached to her right only to
swat at empty air. Same when she reached left.
Whoever was trying to blind her had also stolen
her pillows and shrunk her bed.

Prying open one eye, she found herself face-
to-face with a royal blue wall. Her bedroom was
beige-and-brown. Whose bedroom was this?
More importantly, how did she get here?

Bit by bit, reality worked its way into her brain.
Mexico. Sometime during the night, she'd decided to stare at the stars, and stumbled her way
to the terrace. She must have fallen asleep on
the divan because she lay on her stomach, the

side of her face smashed against a royal blue throw pillow.

How much did she drink? Too much, seeing how her tongue felt like it'd been wrapped in cotton socks. And her head… Thinking made the pounding at the back of her skull worse. Damn Delilah and Chloe for sending her that champagne.

"Why? We weren't the ones filling your glass," her friend Chloe would say, and sadly, she'd be right. Larrissa did the pouring all by herself. Seven hundred fifty milliliters of champagne and half a bottle of Spanish wine worth. She gagged, contemplating the volume.

Wouldn't Tom be thrilled to see her now? After all, wasn't she to blame for everything? Their breakup, his cheating. *She challenges me, Larissa. Makes me think about things. All you talk about is the wedding. It's like you don't care about anything else.*

Apparently he missed the part where planning a wedding was a lot of work. Too busy having deep conversations with the other woman, no doubt.

Letting out a groan, she pushed herself to an upright position and stumbled to the living area, praying the powers that be included an industrial-strength coffeemaker. She still couldn't believe Delilah and Chloe paid to upgrade her to the Presidential Villa. The place was astounding, albeit filled with way too much sunshine at the moment. One glass wall looked out over the ocean, the other onto the lagoon. The entire villa was a glass box with curtains. Ironic since the resort boasted complete privacy.

Where did she put her sunglasses? She could have sworn she had them on her head when she checked in. Without them, her head was going to explode.

Oomph! She forgot the living room had a sunken conversation area. Missing the step, she lost her balance and pitched forward. Fortunately, her hand managed to catch the edge of the sofa. As her fingers curled around the cushion, a memory made its way into her head. Sad brown eyes with thick lashes that sent odd spiraling sensations down her back. *They'd talked about rela-*

tionships. He said he was a widower. She said she was sorry for his loss and...

And she touched him.

Oh, Lord, please say she did not come on to a complete stranger last night. A quick look at the open wine bottles said it was entirely possible.

A knock on the door sliced her head open. "Room service," an accented voice called out.

Peering through the peephole, Larissa spied a cart laded with silver serving pieces as well as—heaven help her—another bottle of champagne—and groaned. The wedding day breakfast package. She must have forgotten to cancel.

"For the bride," the server announced when she opened the door. He very diplomatically pretended not to notice her appearance, but Larissa caught the sideways glance as he wheeled the cart inside. Whatever. No different from the looks she got checking in. Single definitely stuck out at La Joya. Combing her fingers through her hair, she smiled brightly, as if she woke up wearing yesterday's clothes and smelling of stale wine every morning. Damn, but those sunglasses would definitely come in handy about now.

Dish by dish, the server unveiled the contents of each platter. Fresh strawberries. Whipped cream. *Huevos motulenos* with plantains and peas. Their aromas mingled together into one fruity, spicy fragrance. Larissa's stomach rose in her throat.

"Is there coffee?" she interrupted before the man could unveil the final dish, which she was pretty certain would be bacon. The greasy scent would send her right over the edge.

"I can serve myself," Larissa continued when he reached for the thermal pot.

Her upright quotient was nearing its end, and she didn't want to waste what little standing ability she had left on some elaborate presentation. Scribbling her room number on the bottom of the bill, she thrust the paper in the man's hand and hoped the generous tip would balance out her curt behavior.

"Please tell the chef everything looks wonderful." She swallowed hard to get the words out. "Exactly as advertised."

"I'm glad you think so," a new voice replied. Before she could reply, the man from her memories strolled into the room. Tall, dark and way too crisp-looking.

Her vague memories didn't do him nearly enough justice. Broad shoulders. A hard, lean body. Her fingertips tingled recalling the feel of his torso all too clearly. Especially the way her palm spread against the taut muscles.

It was his face she'd forgotten. Hidden by the distraction of sad eyes was a face marked by character. A strong jaw, a prominent nose. Skin the color of burnished gold. It was a rugged, masculine face, carved to capture both attention and respect.

He greeted her with a polite nod. "*Buenos dias,* Señorita Boyd."

Dammit, she'd forgotten his name. He wasn't the kind of man a person forgot, either. Maybe if she smiled brightly enough, she could fake her way through the conversation until it came to her. "*Buenos dias.* How are you doing this morning?"

"I am fine, señorita. A more important question is, how are you?"

"Right as rain," she lied.

He arched his brow, proof she wasn't fooling

anyone, but chose to turn his attention to the room service cart. Larissa couldn't help but notice the server's nervousness regarding the inspection. Señor Whoever-He-Was must run a tight ship.

"You're having the bridal breakfast, I see," he said finally.

"Yes, I am."

"Interesting choice. Did you mean to?"

An odd question, although she'd been kicking herself over its appearance herself. She waited until he'd dismissed the server before asking, "What do you mean?"

"Only that considering your circumstances, I'm surprised you're interested in having the full bridal morning experience."

Was he referring to her hangover or the fact she was no longer a bride? His diplomatic description made it hard to tell.

He uncovered the bacon. A big mistake. Larissa started to gag.

"I'm looking forward to it," she replied, swallowing her stomach back into place. Easier than swallowing her pride, apparently. "No sense letting a good meal go to waste."

"I applaud your attitude. Personally, I wouldn't be able to look at food, let alone eat so much."

Okay, so they were talking about her hangover. "I have an iron stomach."

Again, he raised his brow, unconvinced. They both knew she hammered herself into oblivion last night. Only a fool would insist on pretending otherwise. Call her a fool then. And would have to salvage pride where she could. Especially considering her only clear memory from last night involved falling against that hard, lean chest.

"You have a far better constitution than I do," he remarked. "Cream and sugar? Or do you prefer your coffee black?"

What she would prefer would be if he—and the breakfast cart—left her alone so she could collapse. "Black, please."

"I have to warn you, Mexican coffee is brewed stronger than American. Many of our guests are taken by surprise."

"I'm willing to take the chance." Anything to hurry him out of her room. What was he doing here anyway? Her fingertips started to tingle again. Oh, no. Maybe she did come on to him, and he was here because he thought she wanted some kind of Mexican fling.

"While you are here, you must try our version of *café de olla*. We brew the coffee with cinnamon and *piloncillo*. It's sweet, but not overly so. The secret is in using the right pot."

"Uh-huh." She was far more interested in getting through this cup of coffee. Those stainless steel covers didn't do much to contain aromas, did they? His nattering on about brown sugar didn't help. Between the two, her stomach was pretty much ready to revolt. If she didn't know better, she'd swear all his talk was on purpose, to test how long she could hold on before cracking.

"Do all your guests get such personal service from the general manager, or am I one of the lucky ones?" Assuming he was the general manager; she could be promoting him in her head. Drat, why couldn't she remember his name?

His chuckle as she snatched the cup from his hands was low and sultry, making her stomach list. Well, either the sound or the champagne.

"I suppose you could consider yourself lucky. Normally, our wedding director meets with our bridal guests."

"But you don't have one," she replied. Another piece of last night's conversation slipping into place.

The coffee smelled horrible. Apparently, the resort considered *strong* a synonym for *burnt*. Holding her breath, Larissa lapped at the hot liquid. The acidy taste burned her esophagus before joining the war in her stomach.

Check that, the coffee was still debating whether it wanted to join. She put the cup on the desk.

Meanwhile, her dark-suited guest was helping himself to a cup. "That's correct," he said. "We are in between coordinators at the moment. Which is why I'm making a point of working with our VIP customers personally. I want to make sure their experience with us is exactly as they anticipated."

"Little late there," Larissa replied. This trip already wasn't what she expected.

Realizing his *faux pas,* the manager cleared his

throat. "That is why I decided to visit you first. I noticed—"

Carlos! His name rushed back. Unfortunately, so did the coffee. Larissa grabbed a nearby waste bucket.

And promptly threw up.

CHAPTER TWO

"ARE YOU FEELING better yet?" The voice on the other side of the door rolled far more gently than Larissa's stomach.

"Yes," she managed to croak. After her embarrassing display with the waste bucket, she wasn't about to admit anything else.

Happy Wedding Day to me. Her big day. The moment she'd dreamed about her whole life, when the world would see that she, little Larissa Boyd, found her Prince Charming. No more pinning sequins on someone else's wedding gown or standing in the sidelines.

Never, in all her dreams, did she see herself sprawled on Spanish tiles with her head propped against a walk-in shower.

Dammit, Tom.

"Do you need anything?"

Something to put her out of her misery might be nice. "I'm fine. I need a few minutes is all."

"Are you sure?"

"Positive. There's no need to for you to hang around. I'll be fine."

She listened for sounds of his departure, but heard none. You'd think he'd take advantage of her locking herself in the bathroom to get as far away from her as possible. Was he that afraid she'd pass out and bang her head?

Struggling to her feet, she wobbled to the sink. Shaky as her mind was, she was still able to appreciate her surroundings. The room was so large, you could fit three of her bathroom back home—one in the sunken tub alone. Needless to say, at the moment she could do without all the sunlight. What was it with this place and windows? Brightness poured in from all angles, bouncing off the glass accessories in near blinding proportion.

Too bad she couldn't keep her eyes closed forever. Crawl under the covers and start the day over. One look at her reflection, however, and she wondered if simply starting the day over would be enough. No wonder the room service guy looked at her askance. She looked like a rabid blue-eyed raccoon. Grabbing a tissue, she swiped at her eyes, succeeding only in spreading the smudges to her temple.

"Señorita?"

On top of everything, he wouldn't leave. Señor Chavez. No way she'd forget his name again. Although she'd bet he'd like to forget hers. In less than a day she'd gotten drunk, flirted with him and gotten sick in the wastebasket.

So much for being a VIP guest.

Clearly he wasn't going away until she showed her face, so she might as well drag herself outside. With a heavy sigh, she gave one last useless swipe at her mascara, and reached for the door.

Señor Chavez stood looking out to the lagoon. Meaning his back was to the room, thank goodness. She needed to work her way up to looking him in the eye. As it was, his black-suited presence filled the room with an awkward tension.

Interestingly, she could no longer smell the food. Her breakfast had disappeared.

"I moved the service cart outside," he said. "I

know how overwhelming certain aromas can be when you're feeling under the weather."

And yet, he'd made a production of serving her coffee. She'd been right; her little pretense didn't fool him one bit. If she weren't about to die, she'd be annoyed.

"And the waste bucket?"

"Outside as well. Housekeeping will bring you a fresh one later today."

"Thank you," she said, annoyance taking a back seat to manners. Whether he'd been testing her or not, she had no one to blame but herself for her condition, and they both knew it.

He glanced at her from over his shoulder. "Your bag rang while you were indisposed as well."

Took a moment to realize he meant her cell phone. "My friends checking in to make sure I arrived safely." Had to be. Delilah and Chloe were the only two people in her life who cared. Grandma was gone and Tom...well, like he'd call.

"The same people who paid for your upgrade?"

"And the champagne." The enablers. "I don't normally drink so much," she told him, figuring she should at least try and explain her sorry state. "Let alone on an empty stomach. It's just that last night, I was sitting here..."

When it struck her, she was on her honeymoon alone. What back in New York seemed like such a grand gesture of independence suddenly felt pathetic. And so she figured, why not indulge in a good old pity party?

"I guess I was feeling vulnerable," she told him. "Today was supposed to be my wedding day."

"I know. You told me last night."

"That's right, I did." She always did over share with strangers when she'd had a little too much to drink. Chloe used to tease her about how she practically shared her life story the day the two of them met, and that was after a few glasses of wine in a bar after their corporate orientation. Who knew what a bottle of Cristal made her babble? "Did I say anything else?"

"You don't remember?"

"For the most part I do." A small white lie. She remembered thinking the space didn't feel quite so empty once he arrived, and the way his five o'clock shadow had felt rough against his fingers. "There are a couple blank spots, though. I didn't do anything…embarrassing, did I?" Like come on to him? A flashing image of brown eyes looming dangerously close set her stomach to churning again.

"I left the coffee in case you needed the caffeine," he said. A neat change of subject that was answer enough. Inwardly, Larissa cringed.

"Would you like me to pour you a fresh cup?"

"No, thank you." She couldn't take the burnt smell for a second time. "I think I'm better off with something cold. Maybe one of those twenty-dollar colas from the mini-bar." A few dozen pain relievers would be nice as well, she thought, combing her fingers through her hair. "I don't suppose these rooms also come stocked with aspirin."

"Next to the coffeepot."

Sure enough, a bottle of pills sat on the desk, next to the thermos. They hadn't been there before. "I suspected you might need them."

"Thank you."

"You're most welcome. We strive for nothing less than one hundred percent satisfaction from all our guests. You said cola, correct?"

"That's not…" Before Larissa could utter a protest, she'd crossed the distance between terrace and cabinet. "Necessary."

"Of course it is. You're my guest. It's my job to make sure you're happy."

Although Larissa knew she was but one of a thousand guests, his lilting tone made the comment sound far more personal. As though she were the only one getting such hands-on treatment. She blamed her condition for the nervous fluttering in her stomach. "Even the hung-over ones?"

"Especially the hungover ones," he said popping open the can.

Larissa felt her cheeks flush. "My friends always did say I was high-maintenance."

"Are you?"

Good question. It always struck her funny, how her New York circle gave her that reputation. Growing up, she'd perfected the art of staying out of the way. Expensive dresses and "sticky kid stuff" didn't mix, according to her grandmother. If she was going to live there, Larissa had better learn to be careful.

"I prefer the term *particular,*" she replied.

Naturally, the universe decided to deflate her argument by tangling their fingers when Larissa reached for the soda can. The contact shocked her, so much so she jerked the can from his grip with a gasp. "I—um." She looked up in time to catch something—a light but not quite a light—flashing in his brown eyes. One blink and it disappeared. Hidden behind a polite, distant shade. Didn't matter. Even if she hadn't seen anything, the way his body stiffened at the contact was message enough. She did them both a favor and stepped back. "Are you sure I didn't do or say anything stupid last night?"

"Nothing that bears repeating."

But something, nonetheless. Enough that her proximity made him uncomfortable. Great, she thought, cringing. Probably best that she not to press for details. "I'll do my best to stay under the radar for the rest of my visit. In fact, you'll barely notice I'm here," she added, taking a drink. Raising the can blocked her from seeing any skepticism.

On a positive note, the cold fizz felt wonderful

on the back of her throat. Didn't completely wash away the cotton sock taste, but helped.

"Speaking of your stay, Señorita…" Reaching into his breast pocket, he removed a neatly creased sheet of paper. "I had some questions about your itinerary, now that your original plans have…"

"Bitten the dust?" Larissa supplied. "And please, call me Larissa. Formality seems a little silly at this point, don't you think?"

A hint of a smile played at the corner of his mouth. "Very well, *Larissa.* According to our records, you booked a number of activities for while you're staying with us."

Larissa remembered. The wedding coordinator made everything sound so wonderful over the phone. Unable to pick one or two, she selected everything. *You only get one honeymoon,* she'd rationalized. Why not make it as romantic as possible?

"I'm assuming you are no longer interested."

"You assume correct." Moonlight dinner cruises and couples massages weren't exactly solo activities. "The only activity on my schedule this week is following the angle of the sun." And hopefully figuring out what caused her perfect engagement to implode so spectacularly. *See, Tom, I am capable of introspection.*

Out of the corner of her eye, she caught the manager looking at his paper. "What? Is there a problem?"

"Not at all. I'll make sure all your previous events are canceled. Although you realize, by canceling at such short notice, you are respon—"

"Wait, wait, wait. Short notice? I canceled everything weeks ago."

He frowned. "Not according to our records."

"Well, your records are wrong." It would take more than a couple bottles of wine to erase that phone call from her memory. "What did you think I was going to do? Marry myself?"

"I assumed you didn't realize the wedding was off last night."

A logical assumption. Wrong, but logical. "I spoke to your wedding planner six weeks ago."

"Six weeks." He inhaled deeply. "Are you sure you spoke directly with Maria del Olma?"

"Positive, and she assured me canceling wouldn't be a problem."

Except apparently it was, if his quivering jaw muscle was any indication. "It appears there's been a miscommunication. Maria never noted the cancellation in your records."

"Well, I'm noting it now."

"I don't suppose you have written confirmation."

Larissa started to say yes, only to snap her mouth shut. Come to think of it, Maria didn't send any follow-up. Normally, Larissa would request a letter for her files, but she'd been so upset she must have let it go. Plus, Delilah was getting married, and Chloe was having relationship drama. Following up slipped her mind.

Could she start this whole trip over? Please?

Turning on her heel, she stomped onto the terrace. Sunshine and brightness be damned; she needed fresh air. In keeping with the morning's theme, she bumped into the lounge chair, stubbing her toe on a piece of plastic. Her missing sunglasses skidded across the floor. Score one positive. She shoved them on her face as she limped toward the railing.

At least the view remained as beautiful as she remembered. Unlike in New York where activity reigned 24/7, the day had yet to get started. The lagoon's surface was an aqua-green mirror, the only sign of visible life a solitary egret stalking the opposite shore. Occasionally the leaves in the upper canopy would rustle as an unseen bird, or monkey maybe, alighted from a branch. After four years of city living, Larissa forgot such serenity existed.

She remembered when she decided to get married at La Joya. The photos online looked so gorgeous, she'd fallen in love at first sight. What could be more romantic than getting married in paradise? Delilah and Chloe always teased her when she said stuff like that. *You think everything's romantic,* Delilah would say. Then they'd joked and call her a Bridezilla because she changed the venue three times.

She loved her friends, but they didn't understand her any more than Tom did. She'd been planning her wedding day since she was six years old, and spied on her first dress fitting through the crack in her grandmother's accordion doors. When the bride stepped out of the fitting room all white and sparkly, it was like a princess in real life. So pretty, so…special. Standing there, surrounded by faded yellow wallpaper, she glowed. They all did. All the brides, all the prom queens. Delilah did, too, when she married Simon. So much so, it took her breath away. All Larissa wanted was to glow like that. To have one day where she was the princess.

And she'd come so close. She could still remember how excited she'd been when Tom proposed. Handsome, successful, stable Tom Wainwright wanted her. All those years dreaming a man would fall in love with her, and whisk her off into the sunset and finally her dream had come true. Or so she'd thought.

A soft cough reminded her she wasn't alone. Señor Chavez had moved to her elbow. "I'm told our former wedding coordinator was quite distracted toward the end of her tenure with us. Her abrupt departure has caused more than a few loose ends."

"Let me guess. She left six weeks ago."

"I'm afraid so."

Figures. How much did Larissa want to bet she took off shortly after their phone conversation?

"I'll personally take care of canceling all your obligations. However, there is one problem."

Say no more. Larissa made her living typing advertising sales contracts. An agreement was an agreement. Without evidence she actually spoke with Maria del Olma, it was her word against the computer system. "You're telling me I'm liable for the expense. How much?" She tried to remember the terms of their agreement. Technically, she gave them fewer than twenty-four hours. Which meant...

There was a pause. "The entire amount."

Oh for crying out loud. "Seriously? The whole thing?"

"I am afraid so."

"Even though you guys are the ones who made the mistake." She shook her head. If she ever found Maria del Olma, she would slap the woman. No way Tom would pony up any of his share, either. She could hear him now. *This was your obsession, Larissa, not mine.*

"You know this is completely unfair, don't you?"

"I'm sorry."

"You can't take something off the bill?" After all, it was his staff member's error.

"Please?" she asked, lowering her glasses. She could tell from his expression, he was struggling with a response, the need to recoup costs clashing with his desire to make the guest happy. Might as well throw a little hangdog-inspired guilt in to tilt the scales in her favor. "What if I pay half?"

He sighed. "Best I can do is reduce the cost by thirty percent."

"Only thirty?" This was so not helping her headache. "What about the fact that I brought in business? Didn't you say those people signed a contract?" In her opinion, she deserved half off for that alone.

A shadow crossed the railing as he appeared at her elbow. Looking right, she saw him studying her with an arched brow. "I thought you didn't remember last night."

"I remember the reason for the Cabernet." In fact, she was pretty sure she toasted the couple's health and happiness once or twice.

"The Steinbergs are the reason I'm willing to go as high as thirty."

"Oh."

"You have to understand, space was blocked off, food has been specially prepared. The bridal cake alone…"

"No need to explain. I get it." She'd heard the sales department make similar arguments every day. Legal contracts didn't care about your sob story.

"I am sorry."

Not as sorry as she was. "What's going to happen to everything I ordered?" The custom-colored linen, the custom spa arrangements. Her headache doubled as she thought of all the little extras. She couldn't begin to list everything.

"What can be returned to venders will be returned, the rest, like the food, will be served through the restaurant or sadly, thrown away."

"Including the cake?" Her beautiful, three-tier white chocolate cake with raspberry mousse filling.

"I suspect it will become tonight's dessert special."

"Well, isn't that peachy? I can order my reception dinner and pay twice. I might as well go ahead and have the reception anyway."

He stared, clearly trying to read whether she was serious. "Aren't we being a bit extreme? It is, after all, only a dinner."

"Only a dinner?" No, chicken in a bucket was only a dinner. This was fifteen months of work and planning. "We're talking about my wedding reception."

"Which, had it taken place, would have had you marrying a man who was unfaithful."

Larissa winced. "Thanks for reminding me."

"Better to see things clearly now than stay lost in a romantic haze only to discover the truth five months later," he replied. "Trust me, a dinner is a far easier price to pay."

"Reception," Larissa corrected under her breath. There *was* a difference. Clearly, he thought her as silly as everyone else. Maybe they were right, and she was silly and overly romantic. Didn't make today sting any less.

"I think I'm going to lie down," she said with a sniff. "My head feels like it's going to explode."

"Of course. I'll make sure housekeeping doesn't bother you," he said, moving toward the door. "Again, I am sorry for the miscommunication."

"Thirty percent sorry, anyway," she replied.

A small smile tugged at his mouth, but was quickly reined in. "I hope you feel better."

"Me, too," she told him, turning back to the view. Paradise had suddenly become very expensive.

So help him, if Maria del Olma or her boyfriend ever stepped foot on resort property again, he would strangle both of them with his bare hands. Teeth clenched, Carlos let out a low growl, and wished he was farther away from Larissa's front door so he could growl louder. He knew his predecessor and the coordinator left the resort in chaos, but he'd thought they'd caught the worst of the errors weeks ago. Apparently he thought wrong.

At least housekeeping did its job and spirited

away both the waste bucket and room service cart while he was having his awkward discussion with Señorita Boyd. Guests might want to overindulge in Mexican paradise, but they didn't want to see the morning-after evidence. Señorita Boyd's—Larissa's—villa wouldn't be housekeeping's only stop. There would be a number of guests looking for dry toast and aspirin this morning.

But only one had the aspirin delivered personally by the general manager. Then again, none of the other guests invaded his thoughts all night long, either. He couldn't shake the image of her alone in her suite, drinking away a broken heart, to the point that when he woke up this morning, the first question in his head was how she fared.

The answer was about as he expected. The results of an alcohol-fueled pity party were never pretty. She looked like death warmed over, yesterday's sex appeal all but obliterated. To her credit, she tried, pretending her skin wasn't turning green while he talked about coffee. She lasted longer than he thought she would. Then, to work up the energy to negotiate her bill, as well. Admirable.

Too admirable seeing how he agreed to absorb thirty percent of her expenses. What came over him, making such an agreement? There were concessions and then there were concessions.

You know exactly what came over you. You looked into those big blue eyes and wanted nothing more than to make them sparkle.

Nonsense. He felt sorry for the woman, that was all. He knew all too well the pain of waking up and realizing you'd been living a delusion. And to have the covers ripped from your eyes so quickly… His own disenchantment unfolded slowly, and that pain was bad enough.

What would have happened if he'd realized the truth about Mirabelle from the beginning? Would he have still spent so much energy trying to make her happy? Probably. He'd been such a stubborn, romantic fool back then. Quick to fall, slow to let go.

Thank goodness he'd learned his lesson since then.

"*Hola, primo!* I've been looking all over for you."

His cousin, Jorge, jogged toward him. Like

Carlos, he wore a black suit, although in Jorge's case, the jacket fit snugly around his barrel chest, a fact his cousin, an American football player at UCLA, took great pride in. "You do realize the resort has a perfectly good boat launch that allows you to cover the ground in half the time," he said, wiping the dampness from his upper lip.

"The boat launch doesn't allow me to see the beach side of the resort. You might want to consider walking this route yourself. You're out of breath."

"Because I've been walking all over the property looking for you. Where have you been? You missed morning coffee."

"I was meeting with a guest."

"At this hour of the morning? Don't tell me you're picking up Rodrigo's bad habits."

Upon hearing his predecessor's name, Carlos's muscles tensed. "I was meeting with La— Señorita Boyd—regarding her wedding plans."

"Boyd. Isn't she the woman who checked in by herself yesterday?"

"She is. Maria forgot to cancel her wedding ceremony."

"You're kidding."

"I wish I was," Carlos replied with a sigh. "It appears she was too busy sneaking around with Rodrigo to let catering know. I had to break the bad news to Señorita Boyd this morning."

"You're not charging her, are you?"

"What choice do I have? Everything was ordered, and you know as well as I do the resort isn't in a position to eat those kinds of costs right now. I gave her as much of a discount as I could."

That he even had to conduct such a negotiation made him want to rip his hair from his head. "Sometimes I don't know who I want to strangle more. Maria for being so careless or Rodrigo for mismanaging the resort into financial crisis."

"I thought that's why I came aboard. To give you an extra set of hands so you could strangle both simultaneously."

This was one of those rare days when Carlos wanted to take his cousin's joke seriously. "I need you to have someone go through every event Maria booked. Call the people and update their contracts. I do not want a repeat problem."

"I'll take care of it soon as we get back to the office."

"Thank you. Meanwhile, let's hope the wedding coordinator candidate I'm interviewing this afternoon is more levelheaded."

"He's male, so at least we won't have to worry about the two of you running off together."

Carlos ignored the remark. Wouldn't make a difference if the candidate was male or female. His days of losing his head were long gone and they both knew it. "Have you checked on the Campanella arrangements yet this morning?" he asked instead.

His cousin nodded. "Everything's running on schedule."

"Bueno."

"The señor and the señora did ask if you'd be willing to make a toast. Apparently someone they know was toasted by the captain of a cruise ship."

"And they would like something similar." Carlos thought of Larissa asking about her cake. "So many silly details. As if any will matter six months or even six hours later."

"It would mean a lot to them."

"Then I'll be there." Whatever a guest wanted. Especially guests like the Campanellas who seemed the type to leave online critiques. He wondered if Larissa Boyd left critiques? What would she say? The general manager efficiently provided aspirin?

"What's so amusing?"

He didn't realize he'd chuckled aloud. "Nothing.

"Uh-huh. Is everything all right, *primo?* You seem distracted this morning."

"Of course I'm distracted. I thought we were finished mopping up Rodrigo's and Maria's messes. Instead I had to bill a jilted customer on her wedding day."

"Better you than me. I would have caved completely out of sympathy."

Carlos didn't say how close he came to doing that very thing. The two of them fell into step back to the office. Although only midmorning, the sun already hung hot in the cloudless sky. Sunbathers, eager to turn their skin to Aztec gold, crowded both sides of the walkway. A mosaic of body shapes sprawled towels and chaise longues. Some of the more cautious tourists staked their claims on the popular cabana beds scattered strategically around the resort. He wondered, would Larissa Boyd find her way to one of them to sleep off her hangover or would she prefer the privacy of her terrace? Pale skin like hers would definitely burn if exposed too long.

"I have to admit," Jorge continued, "now that you tell me the wedding was canceled weeks ago, I'm surprised she's here. She must have had nonrefundable airline tickets."

"Or perhaps she simply needed to get away." He understood. After a while, all the well-meaning comments and sympathetic looks started to eat at your soul. It was either scream at people to go away or lose yourself in a place full of distractions. "Whatever her reason, ours is not the place to judge."

"The staff is fascinated by her. She made quite a memorable impression yesterday."

Blue smudged eyes and rat nest hair came to mind. Memorable indeed. Wonder what Jorge would say if he saw her this morning.

Interestingly, he was beginning to think this morning's version might be more memorable.

Mirabelle used to worry incessantly about her appearance, obsess over every hair, every ounce on her frame. As much as he reassured her that she would be the most beautiful woman in the world to him, his reassurances fell on deaf ears. Fell, and fell, and fell.

Something in him wanted to hope Larissa Boyd was different. Stronger.

"I don't think we've ever had a guest stay solo before." Jorge's voice saved his thoughts from traveling down a dark road.

"Of course we've had single guests," he replied.

"Single, yes, but always as part of a group. I can't remember ever having someone attend completely alone before. Certainly not a woman on her honeymoon."

"There's a first time for everything. Perhaps Señorita Boyd will spark a trend."

"Wouldn't that be nice?" Jorge grinned, his smile white and even. "We could become the new singles hot spot on the Riviera."

"You'd like that, wouldn't you? A hotel full of heartbroken women."

"What is it the Americans say about getting back in the saddle? Perhaps our señorita could use a stirrup."

The idea of his muscular cousin touching pale American skin stuck hard in his chest, giving him heartburn. "The señorita came to nurse a broken heart. I doubt she's interested in riding lessons."

"You never know. Not everyone—"

"Not everyone what?" Carlos whipped around.

"Nothing."

As if Carlos didn't know what he was going to say. *Not everyone grieves forever.* Of anyone in the family, he expected Jorge to understand.

"It's just…" His cousin's voice softened. "It's been five years. Don't you think Mirabelle would want you to move on?"

"My days of giving Mirabelle everything she wanted died with her," he replied. Fitting, really. Given all the times he failed her in life, why should his grief be any different?

Besides, he thought, looking out to the Atlantic, if she'd wanted him to move on, she should have left his heart intact. "The only people I care about making happy these days are our guests. In Señorita Boyd's case, that means protecting her privacy."

"Were you worrying about her privacy when you had security checking on her last night?"

Carlos stopped short. He should have known Jorge would hear of his orders. The hotel staff was a small community, and nothing escaped notice. "She'd been drinking. I thought it a good idea to watch out for her."

"Old habits die hard, do they?"

Some did anyway. He thought about arguing the point, and blaming liability for his behavior, but Jorge would see right through the excuse. After all, his cousin knew all about Mirabelle. More, he'd been there the day they found her.

"I didn't want to take any chances. There were too many similarities." More than he wanted to admit.

Before he could say anything, the two-way

radio on his cousin's waist began to crackle. The first sentence was all Carlos needed to hear. "Housekeeping emergency, Presidential Villa."

CHAPTER THREE

"I'M NORMALLY NOT this squeamish. I mean, I live in New York City. I've seen things." But this wasn't some scrambling little roach or scurrying sewer rat.

The maintenance man grinned. "Tarantula," he said.

No kidding, it was a tarantula. One the size of her fist and it was clinging to the bathroom wall next to the bathtub. Larissa shivered, thinking how she'd been sitting on the floor while it had been crawling around. For all she knew, it could have crawled right by her foot. Or her hair. Heebie-jeebies ran across her skin.

All she wanted to do was take a nice long bath, thinking a whirlpool and a jungle view would be exactly what she needed to shake off her pity party and start fresh. Nowhere did her plans include sharing her tub with a man-eating creature.

She looked over from her place atop the double vanity. "Can you get rid of it?"

"*Si.*" Taking a hand towel, the man brushed the offending creature to the floor. Larissa squeaked and tucked her legs beneath her. How was that getting rid of anything?

Suddenly commotion sounded outside. "What happened?" Señor Chavez burst into the bathroom.

Oh, great, he was back. Was the general manager going to witness every embarrassing moment she had this trip? This time he brought a friend along, as well. A second dark-suited man pulled up behind him.

"The radio said there was an emergency." He looked Larissa up and down with a scrutiny that made her wish she was wearing more than the complimentary robe. She tugged at the gap, making sure the cloth covered her legs.

"There was an emergency. I had an unwelcome guest," she replied, pointing toward the floor. The maintenance man had laid the towel on the ground, and the tarantula was crawling onto the cotton surface toward the middle. "I called to have someone get rid of him."

"I'm afraid tarantulas are an unfortunate by-product of sleeping so close to the jungle," the other man replied with a smile. In comparison to Señor Chavez's scowl, it was positively blinding. "Our staff does its best to sweep them off the property, but every once in a while one makes its way into a room. I'm Jorge Chavez, the assistant manager, by the way."

"Pleasure to meet you." Larissa watched as the maintenance man scooped up the towel and spider. "What's he going to do with him?"

"Pedro will release him away from the property. Don't worry, he won't be back."

"I'm more worried about whether he has friends."

"I doubt there are others, but we'll sweep the villa to make sure. Of course, if you're truly uncomfortable, I can arrange for you to move to a different suite."

"No, that won't be necessary." With the spider gone, she was feeling a little braver. Not brave enough to move off the vanity, but braver. "As long as there are no others."

"I'll check the property myself."

"Thank you." She looked to the general manager, who hadn't said a word since bursting on the scene. At first, she blamed the silence on annoyance, but now that she looked closer, she saw that he'd gotten lost in thought. Distance allowed her to see past the shutters, revealing the haunted sadness she remembered from last night. A sympathetic ache curled through her stomach. He didn't seem the kind of man who would look so lost, and yet at the moment, *lost* was exactly the word she'd use.

"I didn't mean to cause a big scene," she said, raising her voice. Partly to let Jorge hear her and partly to shake Chavez from his thoughts. "When I called housekeeping, I didn't expect an entire army to show up."

"We were in the area."

"They said it was an emergency."

Both men spoke at the same time. Because it was the first Señor Chavez spoke since entering, Larissa turned her focus to him. He'd shaken off whatever ghost captured his attention and returned to scrutinizing with such ferocity you'd think she'd committed a crime, rather than been a victim. "It was an emergency to me," she said, defensiveness rising. "You all might be accustomed to finding poisonous spiders in your bathrooms, but I'm not."

"Contrary to popular belief, tarantulas aren't deadly. At best, you'd get a slight fever."

"Good to know. I'll sleep much better knowing if one does decide to bite me, I won't die." His blunt tone surprised her. What happened to the exceedingly polite, do-anything-to-please-the-guest manager she met this morning? This man seemed far more intent in glaring at her. She didn't understand the change, since she swore when he first burst into the room she saw real live fear on his face.

"No sign of any hairy friends," Jorge announced, returning to the doorway. "I'll have Pedro do a more thorough search and wash down the outside walls to make certain. I'm sorry for your discomfort."

"Me, too. Now I'll be looking everywhere for creepy crawlies my entire vacation."

"We can still switch you to a different suite, if you'd like."

"That really isn't necessary." A new room wouldn't stop her from tiptoeing every time she stepped through the door. A thought occurred to her. "Although, I wouldn't complain about having something taken off my bill. I mean, since my ability to relax has been compromised." Laying it on a bit thick, but seeing how she was in the hole for seventy percent of her wedding, every little bit helped. She arched a brow in Señor Chavez's direction, hoping he'd take the hint.

Instead, the man turned and spoke to his assistant in Spanish. Larissa didn't understand a word of their conversation, but she noticed Jorge's expression soften as he touched his boss's shoulder.

"I'm going to find Pedro," Jorge said after a moment. "If there's anything else we can do to make your stay more comfortable…"

"I'll let you know," Larissa replied. She had a feeling she'd be able to parrot the phrase by the end of the week.

"Guess I'm not doing well when it comes to being low-maintenance," she quipped once Jorge left.

The manager didn't crack even the hint of a smile. "I'll take another ten percent off your reception bill."

Looked like she owed the tarantula a thank-you note. "Too bad his friends weren't around. I might have gotten the costs knocked off the bill completely. I'm joking," she added at his continued glare. "Nothing would be worth having five or six of those suckers crawling on my walls. One was bad enough."

"You do realize you were never in any real danger. There was no need to tell housekeeping you had an emergency."

"I didn't." Was that why he was angry? Okay, so her voice might have been high-pitched and panicked-sounding, and she might have asked that they get to her room "right away," but she never used the word *emergency*. "It's not my fault your housekeeping staff takes panicked tarantula calls seriously. Is that why you came back? Because you thought I was in danger?"

"I was told it was an emergency."

A point he seemed incredibly intent on repeating. "*Emergency* could mean anything. It could mean a broken water faucet. What made you think something happened to me?"

He didn't answer. Rather he strode to the large window on the far end of the bathroom. Hands clasped behind his back, he looked out the large window at the mangrove trees waving in the breeze. For a moment, Larissa thought he'd pulled inward again. "How's your headache?" he asked.

"Better. Manageable." What did that have to do with anything?

"And your mood?"

"Well, until Hairy the Spider showed up, I was planning on soaking myself into a better one. Why?"

"You were pretty upset when I left."

"I was annoyed because I'm stuck paying for a wedding I'm not going actually have. Wouldn't you be? I still don't get what that has to do with—" Seeing him wash a hand over his features, a horrible thought hit her. "Don't tell me you thought I—"

"To be honest, I wasn't sure what to think," he said, turning from the window. "When I left you were shaky, upset, stumbling around. Any number of things could have happened. You could have slipped and fallen, cut yourself on a broken glass...."

"Thrown myself off the balcony."

"It's not funny," he snapped. "Distressed people behave unpredictably."

So they did. But, considering his over the top reaction, Larissa had also managed to touch a nerve. She regretted the remark. "I'm sorry."

"I am the one who should be sorry, Señorita Boyd. I overreacted. Hotel managers never like hearing there's an emergency situation. The word is somewhat of a hot button, I'm afraid."

Something about his expression, the way he avoided looking in her direction, said Larissa wasn't getting the complete answer. "Have you ever had a guest...you know?"

"A guest? No."

But someone. He'd avoided her gaze again. Larissa suddenly felt very, very bad about giving him a hard time. "I thought we decided you were going to call me Larissa."

"So we did. And you should call me Carlos."

"Fair deal. Thank you for saving me from the big mean spider, Carlos."

"Housekeeping saved you, but you're welcome anyway," he replied with a smile. Finally. While he didn't look completely relaxed, the shadows had receded from his features. Larissa was surprised to feel her own spine loosening as well.

Suddenly, it dawned on her that she'd held this entire conversation while curled up on the bathroom vanity. Slowly, she straightened one leg at a time, wincing at the stiffness in her kneecaps.

"How long have you been sitting there?" Carlos asked.

"Awhile. I was afraid to move past the spider, so I climbed up here to call housekeeping."

"Tarantulas don't jump."

"I didn't want to take any chances." She swung her legs, trying to get back her circulation. Her joints clicked with the movement, sending sharp jolts across her kneecap. "Looks like I'm going to need that soak more than ever now."

"Would you like some help getting down?"

"I've got it." She scooted her bottom forward, so that when she dropped, she wouldn't land with much force. When she reached the edge, her feet still dangled six inches or so from the floor. "Funny, I remember jumping up with far less issue," she said before sliding to the tile. No sooner did her toes touch down, than her ankles, numb from her sitting on them for so long, turned, causing her to wobble. Carlos immediately grabbed her elbows. They ended up standing hip to thigh. Larissa felt the roughness of summer wool against her skin, a reminder of how exposed she was beneath her robe. One little movement in either direction and the terrycloth would gap open. Warmth rose from the small space between their bodies. It joined with the coolness of his breath at the hollow of her throat, causing goose bumps.

"Are you steadier now?" he asked.

Larissa nodded. "Looks like you were right to worry. I'm not as steady as I thought." More disturbing was the rush of awareness coiling through her system. She couldn't remember ever reacting this strongly to a man's proximity before, not even Tom's, and here she'd reacted to Carlos twice. Afraid of what he'd think about her burning cheeks, she dropped her gaze to the floor.

"Perhaps after your bath," Carlos began.

"Perhaps." She wasn't so sure. Relaxing her muscles when they were already like jelly didn't seem like a smart idea all of a sudden. The solidness of his grip disappeared. Larissa reached back to hold the vanity.

"I'm sorry I gave you a hard time a moment ago. It was very kind of you to be concerned."

"No more than I would do for any guest."

Right. Because his job was to keep guests happy. She didn't know what had her thinking she was any different. "Still, it seems as though you're forever finding me in a bad way. Hopefully from here on in, I'll be—"

"Lower maintenance?"

"Exactly."

"We can only hope." With a curt nod, he turned and left her alone. As quickly as possible, Larissa noted.

One of these times, he was going to leave with a good impression. Thus far, she hadn't done a very good job.

In the meantime, she planned to soak away her hangover. Having indulged in her pity party, it was time to clear her head and figure out how she let things with Tom go so far south.

But, it wasn't Tom who came to mind as she sank into the lavender-scented water. It was a pair of deep brown eyes she'd known for less than twenty-four hours. And a strong touch she could still feel on her skin.

"You have no idea how much this means to me. To us." Paul Stevas played with the straw hat which, until five minutes ago, had covered his auburn curls. "Linda and I didn't get to have a traditional wedding and there's nothing I'd like more than to give her the wedding she always dreamed of."

Carlos studied the man sitting across from him. Kid, really, as he couldn't be more than twenty-one or twenty-two. The young man corralled him as he was crossed the lobby, and asked for help marking his first wedding anniversary. "We're delighted to help," he said. "I promise, this will be the anniversary celebration of a lifetime."

"Linda's going to be so excited. I was afraid because I asked so last-minute...." Carlos swore the boy's eyes were growing moist. "I didn't want to say anything to her until you and I spoke, in case things didn't work out."

"Last minute is never a problem at La Joya. Our job is to make sure you and your wife have the perfect vacation. Give us a day to pull together a basic proposal package for you to work off of, and we can go from there."

"Fantastic." The young man pumped Carlos's hand. "And don't worry about the budget. Money's no object. I want her to have anything and everything she wants."

He better have a big line of credit, then. Granting his true love's every whim could get expensive. And in the end, it wasn't always enough.

Carlos kept his thoughts to himself. Business was business. If Señor Staves wanted to run himself into debt in the name of love, La Joya would gladly take his business. Served as a nice change of pace to rearranging the accounts to keep their vendors happy. Or negotiating bills with sexy blond guests.

He walked Señor Stevas to the lobby, the young man thanking him effusively every step of the way. "You made our vacation," he repeated, enthusiastically pumping Carlos's hand one last time before leaving.

"Nice to see such a satisfied customer."

His shoulder blades stiffened. Silly to think he could avoid Jorge forever. He could only imagine what his cousin thought about the way Carlos rushed to Larissa's villa. Over a spider, no less. What had he been thinking? Contrary to what he told Larissa, he'd heard the term *emergency* used countless times in his career. Never had he rushed to a room the way he did hers.

Not in five years anyway. When he was married to Mirabelle, he rushed everywhere for fear something might have gone wrong.

"Carlos?"

Turning, he saw his cousin helping himself to one of the complimentary water bottles kept at the front desk. "Those are for the guests."

His cousin's reply was to hand him a water bottle as well. "You didn't answer my question. What did you do to make his vacation?"

"I promised him a vow renewal ceremony to end all ceremonies."

"Sounds simple enough."

"Would be, if we had a decent wedding coordinator."

"I take it this afternoon's candidate failed to impress you?"

Busy drinking his water, Carlos could only shake his head. *Impress* was such a subjective term. While qualified, the man lacked imagination. Anyone could slap together menus and hang decorations. La Joya's reputation required someone with passion. Whose events sang with magic and romance and all the other intangibles people were willing to pay top dollar to experience. Thus far, he'd yet to find such a person.

Ironically, once upon a time he would have been that person. Pre-Mirabelle, of course, when he saw everything through a romantic lens. Those days seemed so long ago. When he was young and willing to do anything—be anything—for the woman he loved. He'd fallen for Mirabelle on sight, and from that moment on nothing mattered but making her happy.

Little did he know he'd taken on an impossible challenge. Mirabelle could never be happy, at least not for long. Her demons—and did she have demons—needed, needed, needed. Right up to the end, when, sensing his heart had no more to give, she shattered it to pieces.

Perhaps his past was the problem. Here he was relying on his gut to find a wedding coordinator when he'd used up all his romantic instincts years ago. He hadn't so much looked at another woman since Mirabell's death. Even if his heart were whole, why put himself at risk a second time?

"So what are you going to do?" Jorge's question brought him back to the issue at hand: Paul Stevas's request.

"Have catering pull together a proposal and hope that it's magical enough to please our young guest and his wife."

"Seeing his enthusiasm, I think you're safe."

"Let's hope. He did say money was no object."

"Well, if that's the case, perhaps you should steal Señorita Boyd's ideas. I took a look at her file when reviewing our bookings—which by the way, appear to be in order—she and Maria pulled together quite an extravaganza. Too bad, it won't be taking place."

"Too bad indeed, seeing as how we're now stuck paying for nearly half of it."

"Tarantulas happen. We'd have given the same deal for any other guest."

"Hmm." Carlos tossed his empty bottle into a wastebasket. Did he run to the other guests' rescue?

"Did Pedro spray her foundation? I would prefer we not have to make any further concessions."

"Juanita called it an emergency. You had no way of knowing—"

"Did he spray?" While he appreciated Jorge's effort, he wasn't in the mood to discuss what happened.

"Si."

"Good."

"He also checked her room again. As I suspected, this morning's visitor traveled solo.

Although, if you'd like, I could double check myself."

"No." The vehemence with which he spoke embarrassed him. "I think we've wasted enough of our time on Señorita Boyd's tarantula."

"Right. I'll leave well enough alone, then." His cousin gave him a long look, full of smug double meaning that left Carlos feeling so exposed, he wanted to smack the man.

Instead, he said, "Thank you," and headed back to his office.

He spent the rest of the afternoon with his nose stuck in occupancy reports, desperately hoping to push the morning's escapades from his brain. He didn't like how Larissa Boyd had captivated his attention. The hold made him uncomfortable. At the same time, he couldn't stop thinking about her. If anything, the harder he tried, the more ingrained she became. How sexy she managed to look curled on that vanity. How, when she slid to the floor, her body came so close he'd felt the belt of her robe brushing against his pant leg. The way her lips parted in surprise...

Maldita! What was wrong with him? Larissa

Boyd was but one attractive woman in a resort full of attractive women—a woman who'd been nothing but trouble, he might add. Why the sudden fascination? Had he been living so long as a monk that her innate sensuality had an extra strong grip?

Whatever the reason, he might as well forget getting any paperwork done. It was time for his evening walk anyway. Who knows what emergencies crept up while he was behind closed doors? Half the time, his inspection found the problems before the staff did.

Thankfully, after six weeks of robbing Peter to pay Paul, the resort appeared back on financial stable ground. The last thing they needed was a rash of bad reviews. But then, wasn't that his job? To anticipate and erase problems before guests ever had a chance to complain? Lucky for everyone, guests were the one class of people he could keep happy.

The lobby was quiet when he opened the door. He must have been lost in thought longer than he realized. Gone were the sun-worshippers and sightseers. The soft flop of sandals had been replaced by the click of high heels. Guitar music and laughter drifted through the terrace porticos. The bar was in full swing. Both trestaurants would be, as well. Nighttime had arrived. He gave a few parting instructions to the night manager, and with Paul Stevas's proposal tucked under his arm, set off for the day's final inspection.

He wasn't looking for Larissa Boyd, he told himself as he passed the hotel's open air restaurant. He wasn't. If he was scanning the tables at the open-air restaurant, it was simply to double-check service. Her presence leapt out at him purely by coincidence. How could a man not notice her? She was the only woman dining alone.

What a difference from the woman he left this morning. Gone were the smudged makeup and floppy hair, replaced by a thick blond bob. The strands brushed just below her jawline, the restaurant lighting turning the color silver. Perhaps the lighting was why her skin looked more radiant, as well. The waitperson said something, and she smiled with such enthusiasm, Carlos swore her face glowed.

Before he realized, he was halfway across the dining room floor.

She was gazing out the window when he approached the table. Mindlessly sipping from her champagne glass. A fringed shawl, so delicate a strong breeze would carry it away, covered her shoulders. Every time she raised her drink, the material would slip, revealing a sliver of white shoulder. Not much. Only enough to make you want to see more. Reminded him of the morning's terrycloth robe, modest and tantalizing at the same time. Like this morning, his body reacted appreciatively.

His voice was uncharacteristically hoarse when he spoke. "Enjoying your dinner?"

She turned quickly, liquid spilling over the rim of her glass. "Señor Chavez! You startled me."

"*Lo siento.* I didn't mean to sneak up on you," he said, retrieving the handkerchief from his breast pocket. "And if I'm to call you Larissa, you should call me Carlos."

It dawned on him she was the only guest he'd ever suggested use the familiar term. Oddly, the suggestion felt completely natural. "I take it, our view has claimed another victim."

"Afraid so. I thought my villa cornered the market on beautiful, but I was wrong."

"Paradise through every window."

"For once, the advertising brochure doesn't exaggerate." She slipped the cotton from his fingers with a smile, a little shyer than the one she gave the waiter, but bright nonetheless. "You must think I'm a horrible klutz. Every time we meet, I'm stumbling or something. I swear I'm usually more graceful. Not much, but definitely more than you've seen."

"This spill I'll take the blame for. The others we'll blame the champagne."

"Oh, I blame the champagne for a lot of things, including not seeing my hairy visitor sooner. Cristal definitely does not come up as smoothly as it goes down." His eyes must have flickered to the glass because she hastily added, "Sparkling water. My drinking alone days are finished."

Good to know. Perhaps now she'd stop occupying his thoughts so much.

Or perhaps not, he thought, scanning her length.

Worry certainly wasn't what he was thinking at the moment. "You certainly look like you've re-covered from your ordeals."

"I have, thank you." She handed back his hand-kerchief, now damp. "Amazing what a long soak and a five-hour nap can do for your psyche. I'm ready to start this trip fresh."

"I'm glad. I hope your stay is everything you envisioned."

"Well, that ship sailed six weeks ago, but I do plan to make the most of it. Who knows when I'll get back to paradise?"

There was that smile again. The muscles in Carlos's cheeks tightened, making him realize he was smiling broadly in return. "Well, let's hope it's not too long between trips."

This was the point where he normally moved on, to greet another set of guests, to complete his perimeter check. "By the way, if you haven't ordered yet, I recommend starting with the *ceviche*. It is Frederico, our head chef's, spe-cialty."

"Oh, I intend to. Along with the *sopa de lima* and the *pollo ticul*."

He recognized the menu immediately. "You're having your reception dinner."

"Of course. I planned it. I'm paying for it. By God, I'm going to eat it."

"You're a woman on a mission, then."

"Damn straight. And after dinner, I plan on having two pieces of my cake. Diet be damned."

Just as he hoped, she was stronger than she first appeared. Carlos's appreciation grew stronger. Did she had any idea how attractive a quality resilience could be? "In that case, I hope the meal is everything you hoped for. *Buenas noches.*"

Finally, his legs moved and he took a step toward the next table.

"Carlos, wait." Her fingers brushed his cuff, stopping him in his tracks. Turning, he caught her peering up through downcast eyes, the blue still vivid in spite of the mascara curtain. Her lower lip worried between her teeth. Simultaneously erotic and shy, the gesture turned his entire body alive with an awareness he hadn't felt in half a decade.

"I don't suppose you'd like to join me?" she asked.

CHAPTER FOUR

"Just for a little while. A drink."

Larissa could feel her cheeks getting hotter by the second. She was handling this all wrong. After this morning's "moment" in the bathroom, he probably thought she was hitting on him. His tense expression said as much.

"It would give me the chance to pay you back for all your kindness the past twenty-four hours," she continued, hoping the reason was enough to erase any hint of a come-on. She didn't know why his opinion mattered so much to her, but it did. This morning's tarantula incident clearly touched a nerve, and she hated being the one responsible for bringing up bad memories. She'd spent a good chunk of the afternoon dwelling on the horrible impression she'd made.

When she wasn't flashing upon the way his hands felt gripping her elbows, that is.

Why that moment caused such an intense wave of attraction to begin with was a mystery. After a long soak, she decided to blame a hazardous combination of exhaustion, alcohol and adrenaline. Along with a dose of old-fashioned female appreciation. He was a handsome man, after all.

"There is no need to pay me back for anything," Carlos said. Larissa blamed the tightness she heard in his voice on her imagination. "I was only doing my job."

"I disagree. You went above and beyond, and I'd like to say thank you. Please." She gestured to the empty seat across from her. "Word on the street says the kitchen has an abundance of chicken."

"Well…"

She could hear him weighing the option in his head. "Seeing as I do own thirty percent of the chicken…."

"You mean forty percent, don't you?" she corrected. "Don't forget, I earned an additional ten percent thanks to Hairy the Tarantula."

"Of course, forty percent. How could I forget?" His comment held a hint of humor, however, and he took a seat. Instantly, a waiter appeared with a place setting.

"Wow, I didn't even see him watching the table," Larissa noted.

"You aren't supposed to. We train our staff to be as discreet as possible."

"So as not to disturb the moment."

"Precisely. Our guests like their privacy. Although—" he paused while the waiter poured a glass of water "—there are moments when our staff has been too good at their job."

"I don't understand."

"Put it this way. While my staff members might be discreet, our guests don't always follow the same rules."

Larissa got the picture. "I suppose love and paradise will cause people to get carried away."

"Yes, they will," he muttered into his glass.

Great, she'd gone and said the wrong thing again. Quickly, she rushed on, hoping to erase whatever bad thoughts she'd churned up in his mind. "Luckily, your staff can relax where I'm concerned. There are absolutely no indiscretions on my agenda."

A hint of a smile played on his lips. "Back to practicing low-maintenance, are we?"

"Hey, it wasn't my fault a man-eating spider decided to vacation in my tub."

The waiter reappeared with their appetizers. "I've often heard Americans call *ceviche* the Mexican sushi. Interesting that you picked so many traditional Yucatán dishes for your reception," Carlos remarked as he set down the plates of spiced fish. "Most of our American guests insist on American staples for their big day."

"American food didn't go with my destination theme. I figured why travel all this way and not completely embrace the culture? Consistency makes for a far more memorable event."

"You sound like an expert."

"Nah, just something I learned from my grandmother. She was a seamstress, and always telling brides 'you don't want one bridesmaid sticking out like a sore thumb and ruining the photo.' I figured the same advice applies to the rest of the wedding."

"Interesting logic."

"Thank you." Larissa decided to accept his

remark as a compliment, whether he meant it as such or not.

Almost twelve hours since she saw him last, and, with the exception of his five-o'clock shadow, he looked as darkly perfect as he did this morning. The wear and tear of the day enriched his appearance. The wrinkles in his suit added depth; the stubble gave him a feral edge.

He ate with the same predatory grace that dominated all his movements. The prongs of his fork slipped neatly between his teeth, disappearing as his lips sealed shut, only to slip free a moment later. Larissa had never paid much attention to how a man ate before, but now she found herself following every bite.

"Is something wrong?" he asked suddenly. "You've barely touched your appetizer. Don't tell me after all your effort, you don't like the dish?"

"The fish is delicious. I—" *I was too busy staring at your mouth to eat.* She speared a piece of fish with her fork. "I was thinking how nice it is to have someone to talk with. Privacy is great, but when you're by yourself, things can get a little dull. Let's face it, there's only so much introspection a woman can do." Not that she'd done much at all yet.

Quiet settled between them, as they chewed their food. "Do you mind if I ask you a question?" Carlos asked after a moment.

You had to commend him for politeness. Most people would have gone ahead and asked, the question was so obvious. "You want to know what I'm doing here by myself in the first place."

"Far be it for me to downgrade my own resort, but La Joya is a couples getaway. If you wanted to spend time in the sun, there are dozens of quality Mexican resorts that cater to single guests. Why come here, especially considering you and your fiancé planned...?" He let the question drift away.

"You mean, why pour salt in the wounds by showing up at the same resort where I planned to be married?"

"Exactly."

Where did she start? Setting down her fork, Larissa folded her hands in front of her and tried to put her thoughts in order. Since she'd given the same speech to Delilah and Chloe, the answer should have come easily, but her mind didn't seem to be working the same way today as it had been the past six weeks. "Six weeks ago, I would have said the same thing. Why come here. In fact, I had my hand on the phone the next day, planning to cancel everything. Plane tickets and reservations included."

"What made you change your mind?"

"Michael D'Allesio."

"Who?"

Goodness, but she hadn't said that name in almost nine long years. "He was a boy I knew in high school." Pimply-faced Mike D'Allesio who played trumpet in the band and worked Saturdays at the ice cream shop. He'd always smiled at her when she went to his window to order. "I asked him to go to the prom, and he said yes, only to take Corinne Brown instead."

"He canceled?"

Larissa shot him a look. Clearly he'd never been an unpopular chubby girl. "More like never followed through."

"You mean, he stood you up?" A foreign concept to someone like him, who lived and breathed etiquette.

"Turns out he only said yes because I put him on the spot and he didn't know how to say no."

"So did you go by yourself?"

"No. I sat home and stuffed my face full of cream cheese brownies while wearing my prom dress." She could still see herself, mascara streaking her face, crumbs spilling onto her lap. Such a pathetic scene. The memory left her sick to her stomach.

"I'm sorry."

"It was eight years ago," she said, shrugging. "Anyway, I had the telephone in my hand to cancel this trip when I saw the picture of my wedding gown I stuck on my mirror and I said, 'screw it.' I wasn't sitting home again. At least here I can sit around and stare at palm trees

"Plus I had nonrefundable airline tickets," she added, seeking to lighten the moment. There was only so much pathos a woman could take.

Across the table, Carlos choked on his drink.

"What?" she asked.

"The part about the airline ticket. Jorge suggested that very same reason this morning."

"You and he were talking about me?"

"I talk about a lot of my guests."

"Oh." She felt a tiny thrill anyway. "Jorge… That's the man who arrived with you this morning, right?"

Carlos nodded. "My cousin."

"I wondered when I heard you two had the same last name. I figured you were either related or Chavez is the Mexican version of Smith."

"We came here together about six weeks ago, shortly after the general manager left."

"I thought you lost your wedding coordinator."

"We lost both," he said in a sharp tone. "They ran off together."

"Oh, my gosh, you're kidding. My friend Delilah just married our boss. They fell in love on a business trip."

"I doubt your friend's relationship and this one are the quite same. Unless your boss also left a wife and an infant son behind."

Oh. "I didn't realize. The poor woman."

Larissa's heart went out to her. "And here I thought Tom blindsided me."

"I'm sorry, I shouldn't have said anything. That was inconsiderate of me."

"No, it's okay." At least now, she understood his comments from this morning. "You were right, when you said it's better I found out before the wedding.

"Funny thing is, I didn't stop to think there might have been a wife when you said they ran off. I assumed they were soul mates."

"More like partners in crime," he said, signaling for the waiter.

"Or both."

"You're joking."

"Look, I'm not saying they were right or even that they're nice people, but love is unpredictable. The heart wants what the heart wants."

"You're far more generous than I am. Considering your own story, I would have thought you'd be far more bitter."

The waiter arrived to clear their plates. Grateful for the interruption, Larissa watched silently as a copper hand lifted away her half-eaten plate. Carlos's comment tapped a can of worms she wasn't ready to deal with yet, including the fact she had yet to feel any real heartache over Tom's leaving.

"What's done is done, right?" she said, when it was once again the two of them. It was the best answer she could muster at the moment. Everything else required deeper explanation, such as accepting that maybe Tom hadn't been the man of her dreams after all. "We can't go back and change the past."

"Unfortunately, we cannot."

Sharpness coated his words, reminding her, too late, that he'd lost his wife. Now it was Larissa's turn to regret her words. She opened her mouth to apologize, only to be stopped by a couple rushing the table.

"We're sorry to interrupt your dinner, Señor Chavez," the man said.

"It's my fault. Paul told me about the vow renewal and I was so excited, I had to say thank you in person."

Carlos introduced them as Paul and Linda Stevas, guests at the resort. "Señor and Señora Stevas want to host a vow renewal ceremony at the end of the week to celebrate their anniversary."

"Congratulations," Larissa said.

Looking at them, she couldn't believe they were old enough to get married, let alone renew their vows. The woman was so waifish and thin, she belonged on a runway. Both her legs together wouldn't make one of Larissa's thighs. Her eyes, which along her lips, took up most of her face, glowed with enthusiasm.

"Thank you," she replied. "I can't wait to hear Señor Chavez's ideas. Paul tells me they're amazing."

"No, I said I'm sure they will be amazing," Paul corrected. "I mean, look around. How can they not, right?"

"Like I told your husband this afternoon, we'll do everything in our power to make sure your anniversary is everything you wish it to be."

Based on the young woman's squeal, neither she nor her husband noticed that Carlos's smooth-as-silk answer lacked enthusiasm. She clapped her hands together. "You have no idea how awesome this is, Señor Chavez. It's, like, a dream come true. I mean, it *is* a dream come true."

"I told you she would be thrilled."

"I'm glad you're both happy," Carlos replied. "We want nothing less here."

"Oh, trust me, we are beyond happy," she assured him. "I don't know if Paul told you, but we didn't have a real wedding…"

"Linda, baby, I don't think we need to go into all that now. We're keeping Señor Chavez from his dinner."

The young woman was so pale, her blush looked crimson in comparison to the rest of her. "When I get excited, I tend to babble."

"I do the same thing," Larissa told her. "No worries. And your husband's right. There's no way you can go wrong with any event you hold here. Whatever you do, make sure you book a private moonlight cruise on the lagoon. The two of you alone under the stars, the smell of mango in the air. It'd be great way to end your trip. Like a repeat wedding night."

Linda blushed again. "That does sound wonderful."

"Can we do that?" Paul asked, looking to Carlos.

"I don't think that will be a problem," Carlos replied.

The pair grinned, then Paul slipped his arm around Linda's shoulders. "Come on, baby. We've taken up enough of Señor Chavez's time. We'll talk more tomorrow."

"They're so sweet," Larissa said after they'd walked away. "Sounds like they're really excited to renew their vows."

"Hmm."

"Is there a problem?" So far as she could see, Paul and Linda were dream guests, eager to spend money and enjoy everything the hotel had to offer. Plus, she did find it sweet the guy wanted to give his wife a fancy anniversary celebration.

"Excuse me. I'm sorry to interrupt again." Paul suddenly appeared back at their table. "But that midnight cruise thing you suggested. Pull out all the stops. I want to make it a night Linda won't forget."

"Of course," Carlos replied. "We wouldn't give you anything less."

"Okay," she said, once Paul was out of reach. "He just became doubly sweet. Doing all this to make his wife happy."

"I only hope he finds everything worth the trouble."

"Why wouldn't he? You saw his wife's face. She's thrilled."

"Tonight. What about tomorrow? Or the week after the ceremony? And if he has to go to this much bother for their first anniversary, what will he have to do for the second to make sure the smile stays on her face?"

"Wow, could you be any more cynical? The two of them obviously eloped, and now the guy wants to indulge his wife. What's wrong with that? You were married. Didn't you oblige your wife now and then?"

"Now and then," he replied.

"See? I rest my case."

"So you do." An odd look crossed his face and Larissa couldn't help but wonder if his concession was more to avoid an argument than because of any point she might have made. There'd been a definite edge to his voice that suggested as much.

"I'm sorry," he continued. "I'm afraid I'm not cut out to be an event coordinator. I was brought here to handle the financial issues, not plan weddings."

There was more to his outburst than being uncomfortable with the job, Larissa was certain of that. She was beginning to think that, for some reason, he had a deep dislike for weddings in general. Rather than press the issue, however, she allowed him his excuse.

"Don't you have a catering manager who can handle these kinds of events for you?"

"You saw what kind of mistakes Maria left us to deal with. My catering manager is already overcommitted handling the events on the books. Asking him to plan a last-minute ceremony in addition to everything else he's doing might cause him to quit. Then where would I be? I will take care of planning Paul's and Linda's event myself."

Larissa nodded at the manila folder that lay by his bread dish. "So is that the work you're bringing home? Their ceremony?"

"It is. I plan to write their proposal after supper."

"What do you have planned?" Like Linda,

Larissa found herself eager to hear his ideas. Probably not for the same reasons, but eager nonetheless.

"Does that include the moonlight cruise you sold them on a second ago?" Carlos asked.

"Yes."

Her request had to wait, because the waiter chose that moment to bring out the next appetizer. Two bowls filled with a pale green broth. *"Sopa de lima,"* he announced. Larissa stirred the mixture with her spoon, letting the citrus smell wash over her. "Tom thought all these details were a waste of money, too."

"I didn't say I thought it a waste of money."

"But you don't think much of all the planning, either. And don't say that's not true," she said, shaking her spoon, "because it's obvious you don't."

She could tell he was choosing his argument by the way he hesitated. "So many people…they spend all this time and effort creating the perfect memory, and for what? So they can pick apart the event after the fact, and focus on the mistakes? Every day, my managers bring me complaints.

The food wasn't what they expected. The temperature in the room was set incorrectly. The service wasn't discreet enough. The service was too discreet. The list is endless.

"Makes me wonder why people even bother," he added, stabbing at his bowl with his spoon. "Especially when no matter what you do, you can't make them happy."

Larissa refrained from comment. The acerbity accompanying his last comment suggested their conversation had crossed from theoretical to personal. Very personal, in fact. She thought of their other encounters. His exaggerated concern this morning, his shuttered expression. Didn't take a detective to realize her host carried some dark, heavy baggage.

Curiosity pushed her to find out what, but she held back. This vacation was about focusing on her own issues, not distracting herself with someone else's. No matter how much someone else's issues cried for her attention.

"Unfortunately for you, Paul and Linda *are* bothering," she said, pointing out the obvious instead. "And from the sounds of things, Paul's looking for spectacular."

"Unfortunately, yes, he is, and if you have any spectacular suggestions, I am more than willing to hear them."

"I am the last person to ask for suggestions. Chloe and Delilah said I was a regular Bridezilla when it came to planning mine."

"Pardon?"

"You know, a wedding monster." One of those very people he'd just described.

For the first time since their conversation began, a small smile tugged at his mouth. "I know," he said, sipping his soup. "I read your proposal."

If she weren't so distracted by the way his lips covered the spoon, Larissa would have been insulted. Damn, but he turned eating sexy. "There's nothing wrong with wanting perfection." She'd given the same argument to Tom and her friends dozens of times.

The smile tugged wider. "If you say so."

"I wouldn't expect you to understand." No one else did. Her ex certainly hadn't.

She turned to stare at the beach. The long

silver-white path that stretched to the horizon. "Did you ever dream of something your whole life only to have it suddenly come true?" she asked. "When that moment does finally come, you want to create this perfect sliver of time. A memory that stands up to all the dreams and wishes. Because you only get one shot at making fantasy reality. If you don't go all out, you'll spend the rest of your life replaying the memory and wishing you'd had."

Her cheeks grew warm realizing how much she'd rambled on. "Anyway," she said, turning back, "that's why people get crazy about their weddings."

Across the table, Carlos was studying her with an indistinguishable expression, his brown eyes sharper than she'd ever seen them. "Go ahead and tell me I'm over the top," she said, tugging her shawl over her exposed shoulders. After all, Tom said that and worse when they broke up. *Over the top, superficial, caught up in the unimportant.* The can of worms she didn't want to open—the one in which Tom might have a point—threatened to raise its lid again.

Eyes yet to leave her, Carlos leaned back in his chair. His long fingers tapped at the file on the table. "So what would you do if you were planning the Stevases' ceremony?"

"Well, to begin with I would…" She stopped when she caught him looking down at the file. "Are you trying to pick my brain for ideas?"

"I merely asked a hypothetical question."

Hypothetical, her foot. "You want me to help you plan the Stevases' recommitment ceremony, don't you?"

"You have to admit, you do have a knack for this sort of thing. First, the Steinbergs, then the Stevases with the moonlight cruise."

"A few suggestions does not a knack make." Although she had to give him credit. At least he didn't try and pretend he wasn't looking for input. "Isn't there a rule about making guests work?"

"A few suggestions does not work make," he replied.

Damn him, for throwing her own retort back in her face.

"Plus," he added "you've already done more work since your arrival than much of my staff."

His tone turned gentle. "I listened to you describe our cruise to the Stevases. You painted exactly the kind of picture they needed to hear. They're looking for magic, and frankly, when it comes to creating magic, I'm…" He paused to study the orchid in the center of the table. "Empty."

"Empty," Larissa repeated. An odd choice of words. It implied that once upon a time he'd had magic. The notion he lost a part of himself made her heart ache.

"All I ask is that you give me a few ideas over dinner. Perhaps things you would have done yourself."

"You want to use my defunct wedding ideas?"

"I want to hear your suggestions. Please. I would consider it a great favor."

Aw, damn, did he have to lean forward so that the candlelight made his eyes sparkle? "What's in it for me?" she asked him.

"Pardon?"

If he was going to ask her to use her wedding to inspire someone else's happiness, she should at least get something out the arrangement. "Seems to me there should be some kind of compensation. Especially since I'm stuck paying for sixty percent of my own failed wedding." The mention of which should be causing more heartache than it was. She truly didn't seem to be missing Tom at all. Again, she slammed the worm can.

Carlos shook his head. "You are asking for me to eat more of the cost."

"Only fair, isn't it?"

He didn't answer. Probably because he had no argument. The business world survived on an unwritten *quid pro quo* of favors. Any good business man would realize that fact. Larissa sipped her sparkling water, and waited for his response.

"Very well," he said, after a moment. "I will erase the wedding charges from your bill."

"Great." Finally, something on this trip was going her way.

"But," he said, tilting his glass in her direction a warning if ever Larissa saw one, "any new expenses you wring up are completely nonnegotiable."

"Fair enough." Getting a tan didn't cost much. What mattered was writing off the past.

She moved her soup to her left and learned forward. "Now, what do you say, we get to work."

"Then, we wrap up everything that evening by sending them on the moonlight dinner cruise I told them about. What do you think?"

"I will have to check on cruise availability," Carlos said, "but other than that, I'd say it sounds terrific. You're a natural at this."

The compliment warmed Larissa more than it should. "Making sure I earn my percentage is all."

"You have and then some. Are you sure you haven't planned events before?"

"Just my wedding," Larissa replied. "Told you, I did a lot of research." Not to mention that, when you spend most of your life fantasizing about something, planning became second nature.

During dinner, Carlos had shifted his chair to the side of the table so they could share the paperwork. He'd shed his jacket, as well.

You'd think the rolled-up sleeves would soften the edge she found so attractive earlier, but a relaxed Carlos was even more alluring. She couldn't blame alcohol or sleep deprivation this time, either. Beneath the table, his knee rested a hair's breadth from hers. Every shift of his body sent the seam of his slacks brushing across her skin. Good thing she had a shawl. Clutching it kept her from breakout in goose bumps.

"Well, your research has paid off for me three times this week," he said, stealing a sip of water. "I don't suppose you want to stay and replace Maria?"

"Why not? I'll chuck my life in New York and move into the Presidential Villa." Talk about the ultimate running away from your troubles. She smirked, waiting for his comeback to her pretend acceptance. What she got was a return grin that made her stomach somersault.

A soft cough broke the conversation. Their waiter hovered by Carlos's elbow, his face a combination of nerves and expectancy. "I'm sorry to interrupt, Señor Chavez, but the rest of the staff wants to know if they could break down the rest of the room."

To her surprise, she and Carlos were the only two people left in the restaurant, the other tables long vacant. So engrossed was she in planning the Stevases' ceremony, she didn't notice the diners coming and going.

"Of course they can, Miguel," Carlos replied. "We'll be out of their way shortly."

"I didn't realize we were keeping your staff from doing their jobs," she said after the server disappeared. "Good thing I decided against having a third piece of cake or they'd still be waiting."

"Would you like—" He had his hand half up, ready to flag Miguel, when she grabbed his forearm.

"Thanks, but I've already had two pieces too many. As it is, I'll have to starve myself tomorrow to make up for the calories."

"Ah, but surely you've heard calories don't count in paradise."

"Tell that to my hips."

"Your hips have nothing to complain about." Her flush must have made him realize how his compliment sounded because she caught a tinge of pink creeping across his cheekbones. His gaze swept downward, to his forearm where her hand continued to rest. She knew she should move, but she couldn't. Like when you touch a hot stove and are unable to pull back quickly despite the sizzle.

Finally, he broke contact with her, sliding his arm free so he could straighten the paperwork. "Thank you again for all your assistance."

"Um, my pleasure." Larissa grabbed her water, hoping to hide her embarrassment. "What else was I going to do tonight? Take myself for a moonlit stroll?"

What Larissa didn't want to tell him was how much she enjoyed his company. Once you got past the stiffness, she discovered he had a very easy way about him. They worked surprisingly well together, too. Carlos was genuinely open to her suggestions, limiting his challenges to budgets and logistics. He contributed a few ideas of his own as well, which surprised her. Not that he had ideas, but the kind of ideas he put forth. For a man who claimed to be "empty" he had a knack for suggesting small, romantic gestures to complement her big picture ideas. More than once, Larissa wondered if his suggestions came from professional or personal experience. Did he, for example, leave orchids on his wife's pillow? If so she'd been a lucky woman, Larissa decided, with a pang in her stomach.

"I'm afraid you may have to take that stroll anyway," Carlos told her. He pointed to his watch. "The last launch departed ten minutes ago."

"It did?" She'd truly lost track of time. "And here I swore tonight I'd get a better night's sleep."

"Fortunately, you're on vacation. Going to bed late is part of the bargain."

"You mean like calories not counting?"

"Exactly." Slipping the papers into their file, he rose to his feet. "I'll walk you back to your villa."

"There's no need. I'm sure I'll be perfectly safe." Wasn't as though she was wandering some anonymous street in Mexico. "If not, I've got pepper spray in my bag."

"I won't ask how you got a weapon through customs," he said with a chuckle. "But I do insist on walking you. Even in the safest of resorts, unexpected accidents can occur.

"Besides," he added, the words coming out low and close to her ear. "It would be rude of me to let you travel unescorted."

Heaven forbid, Larissa thought, tugging at her shawl. With the way his voice sent shivers traveling down her spine, she'd rather the rudeness.

CHAPTER FIVE

"TELL ME ABOUT New York City," Carlos said once they'd left the restaurant. "What do you do there?"

"You mean, when I'm not planning weddings?" She gave her shawl another tug. If she pulled any tighter, she'd choke herself with the silk, but at least the action gave her something to do with her hands. She'd tried leaving them down by her sides, but felt awkward swinging her fingers near the edge of his jacket, like she was waiting for him to snatch her hand in his grip. Larissa wondered if he felt the awkwardness, too, because he had his hand stuffed deep in his pockets.

"I work for an advertising agency," she told him. "Media sales."

"Sounds interesting."

"You're being polite." Media sales definitely

wasn't interesting, at least not to her. "But it pays the bills a lot better than catering."

"Ah, so you did plan events."

"Waitress. Before that, a cashier at a florist. NYU didn't pay for itself. I had to come up with the money somehow."

"You're not from New York originally, are you?"

He stated rather than asked. How they segued from her attending New York University to her hometown, Larissa wasn't sure, although she could guess. Eight years of Big Apple living hadn't completely killed her twang. "I moved there when I was eighteen."

"Because you wanted to attend NYU."

"Because it wasn't Texas." As she expected her answer earned her a look. "In a small town, your reputation is pretty much set at birth," she told him. "I wanted to go some place where I could stretch my wings." Not to mention finding a happily ever after was a heck of a lot easier in a city where you weren't completely surrounded by taller, thinner and blonder. Wasn't as if her grandmother cared if Larissa left; she was glad to be done with her.

"How about you?" Tired of talking about herself, she decided to turn the tables. Maybe in his answers, she'd gain insight into what made him so cynical. "What made you go into the hotel industry?"

"Born into it," he replied. "The Chavez family has a long tradition in the hospitality industry. In fact, my grandfather built one of the first luxury hotels on the Baja peninsula."

"Wow. I'm impressed. Explains how you and your cousin both got sent here."

"You'd be hard-pressed to find a hotel in this country that doesn't employ a Chavez."

"So the name is like Smith."

He chuckled, the warm sound slipping under her skin. "In a way. In addition to being large, we're encouraged to learn the business from the ground up, even if that means working for our competition. My very first job was on the grounds crew for a rival property when I was fourteen years old. You'd be amazed what you can learn about the business weeding gardens. Watch your step."

They reached a section where the walkway stepped down. In spite of the area being well lit, Carlos still reached over and took her elbow. Unlike this morning, when she had a bulky terrycloth robe to protect her, this time his hand touched bare skin.

This was getting ridiculous. There was absolutely no reason for one man to cause this much physical response. Yet here she was, her entire body tingling from the slightest of contact.

"Did your wife work in the hotel business, too?"

He stiffened at the question. *You can't stop poking that nerve, can you, Larissa?* Part of her wondered if she broached the topic on purpose, to distract from the awareness stirring in her stomach.

"Mirabelle was a fashion model," he replied. "We met when I was working a property in California."

That distracted it, all right. Of course his wife had been a model. A man like Carlos, with his magnetic looks and natural virility, would attract only the best. "She must have been very beautiful." Tall, long and leggy, no doubt.

"Yes, she was."

"So you lived in California," she said, shooing away the jealousy that immediately cropped up.

"For a while. Mirabelle had…health…issues so we moved back to Mexico City. I thought being close to her family would help her feel better."

The stilted, practiced tone of his answer unnerved her. He was holding back. Larissa could sense the "but" hovering in the air, the same way she could feel the torment he fought to keep from his voice. All of a sudden, what had been awareness grew into a desire to wrap her arms around him and bring comfort.

She preferred the awareness.

They grew quiet after that. Now more aware of his proximity than ever, Larissa hugged her shawl close to her body. The flimsy material needed anchoring against the sea breeze anyway. She looked across the beach to the ocean which loomed black next to the silver land. Between the moon's brightness and the walkway lights, she could make out the white of the foam left behind each time a wave crashed. "I wonder if the tide is going in or out," she mused aloud.

"Out," Carlos replied. "See the line?" He stopped and pointed to a strip of land where the sand shifted from silver to the color of gray cement. "That is the high tide mark. The sand above the water is freshly wet, which says the water has already been there and is starting to recede."

"I'm impressed. Is knowing the high tide mark part of your job, as well?"

"More a sign that I walk this path too often."

"And how often is that?" she asked.

"Twice a day at least. It's the only way to see what's going on…"

His voice drifted off at the end, along with his attention. Following his gaze, Larissa saw that he'd focused on a shadow up beach, right at the surf line.

"Is that what I think it is?" Looked an awful lot like two people reenacting the famous beach scene from *From Here to Eternity*.

A giggle pierced the night air. Moments later, the shadows became upright and ran toward the villas. Larissa tried hard not to giggle herself. "I see what you mean about forgetting your surroundings. Love and paradise."

"Indeed." From the tension in his voice, the scene made that raw nerve flare again. Had Carlos ever rolled in the surf? *What hardened your heart? Had it been his wife? Her illness?* So many questions danced around her head.

As it turned out, the shadows were staying in the VIP section. Before Larissa realized, she and Carlos had arrived at the beachside entrance to her villa. The pathway ended only a few feet beyond, disappearing into a stretch of silver that became the lip of the lagoon. Larissa could see how the shadows had gotten carried away. With nothing but palm trees and sand, it was easy to feel like the only two people on the planet.

"Thank you for walking me home," she said.

"Thank *you* for staying so late to help me."

She went to smile up at Carlos, only to be attacked by a case of nerves dancing around her stomach. Silly, but all of a sudden she felt like a teenager saying good-night on a date. A part of her knew she should turn and head through the door, while another, stronger part, remained rooted to the spot, capable of little more than swaying back and forth on the balls of her feet. "What time are you presenting your proposal to the Stevases?" she asked.

"Nine o'clock," Carlos replied. "Why?"

"Would you mind if I joined you?"

"You have already given up part of your tri—"

"I don't mind," she interrupted. "I'm invested now. I want to see what Linda Stevas thinks of my ideas." What she didn't want to think about was how the suggestion popped into her head as soon as she realized saying good-night might be the last time she spent time with him this week. "So, do you mind?"

"Not at all. In fact, your presence would be very…welcome."

The way he said the world, rolling it off his tongue, turned the nerves into butterflies. "Then, I'll see you *mañana?*"

"Mañana," Carlos replied. "I am looking forward to it."

His gaze had dropped to her mouth, causing her breath to catch. Larissa rose on tiptoes, compelled by a need to lean closer, only to catch herself before the moment got out of hand. This wasn't a date.

Spinning around, she unlocked her hotel door and slipped inside, clapping her hand over her mouth as soon as she closed the door behind her. What just happened? Had she really been waiting for a good-night kiss?

How long he stood on the walkway after Larissa went inside, Carlos wasn't sure. Long enough for the roaring to leave his ears.

He watched as the light went on in her living room, and when her silhouette appeared in the window, he stepped closer to the building out of her line of sight. The move made him feel improper, as if he were behaving like a voyeur, instead of a man struck dumb by his reactions.

He'd almost kissed her. Staring into her eyes, feeling her body's warmth, he came a breath away from tasting her mouth. Had he lived without a woman in his bed for so long, he could no longer bury his baser instincts? And after all his warning to Jorge about leaving her be. What, he wondered, would she have done if he had kissed her? There was a voice in his head telling him she'd been expecting him to. *Wanted* him to.

Above him, Larissa stood looking outward. Looking for him or staring at the ocean? The angle and shadows combined to hide her expression, so Carlos couldn't tell. Nothing could hide her figure, though. Every contour, every gorgeous curve was on display for the world to see. How on earth could her fiancé find another woman more attractive? And that boy in her high school. Were they both blind? She was... Awareness flared anew. Gritting his teeth, he willed the arousal away. It was the moonlight. The moonlight and all her talk about weddings making him think impractically. Larissa Boyd was recovering from a broken heart. Worse, she was an incurable romantic. He would not take advantage of either. Tomorrow he would be back in control. After all, he wasn't the same lovesick fool he was five years ago. This time he knew the difference between a moment of lust and something more.

For one thing, he couldn't feel "more" even if he wanted to.

* * *

"Señor Chavez! *Buenos dias!*" In contrast to his small size, Paul Stevas's voice boomed through the terrace lounge. Calling out was hardly necessary, as the room was nearly empty. This time of day, the guests who were interested in eating preferred the full-service restaurant or their rooms.

Paul had selected a table overlooking the ocean. Linda was there, too, her short brown hair clipped off her face. In her tank top and shorts, she looked more little girl than married woman. The woman sitting beside her, however… Thanks to her curves, Larissa's navy striped shirt and white shorts looked far more alluring than they were meant to be. Carlos's body reacted immediately, nearly stopping him in his tracks. Unwelcome, but not completely unexpected. He already decided last night that daylight would do little to dilute her appeal.

"My apologies for being late. The staff meeting ran over." Doing his best to ignore the bare leg swinging in his peripheral vision, he put on his best smile. "I trust you haven't been waiting long."

"Only a few minutes," Paul replied. "Larissa has been sharing some of her ideas with us."

"Is that so?" he asked, taking a seat across from her. Took some effort, but he managed not to drop his eyes to her lips.

Color seeped into her cheeks nonetheless. "I was telling them how we thought, since this was an anniversary celebration and not an actual wedding, they might prefer something untraditional," she told him.

He sat and listened while she described La Joya's version of the Mayan wedding ceremony. A beachside ceremony that involved offerings to the four points of the compass. He'd always considered the ritual more gimmick than following true culture, but Larissa wove the details into a magical ceremony of love and commitment even the most traditional of shamans would love. No wonder the Steinbergs couldn't wait to sign a contract. Her enthusiasm was infectious. There was no bitterness, no reluctance in her voice to give away the fact that many of her suggestions came from her own ceremony. His admiration grew.

"What do you mean purify?" Paul asked, interrupting the spell. "Do you mean with a smoke?"

"More like incense," he supplied. "The shaman will add copal to the altar fire. It emits an aroma that smells very similar to frankincense. Usually he waves the smoke around the participants before allowing them to approach. That way you are 'presentable' to the gods." He didn't go into the rest of the ceremony. It largely consisted of mystical elements best left experienced. In a true Mayan ceremony, the shaman would also make a ritual sacrifice. Thankfully, the mystic La Joya used was modern and wise enough to substitute a bloodless sacrifice instead.

"Once the shaman finishes the ceremony, he'll declare you officially committed to one another and your guests will commemorate the moment by showering you with flower petals," Larissa finished for him. "What do you think?"

The young couple exchanged a look.

"Everything sounds wonderful," Linda said. "Beautiful."

"But?"

"It's the incense," Paul said. "I get the point of

the whole purification ceremony, but we don't want any smoke."

"None at all?" There was no mistaking the disappointment in Larissa's voice. Modern or not, all shaman insisted on purification rituals. Vetoing the incense meant vetoing her entire proposal. To his surprise, Carlos found himself disappointed on Larissa's behalf. Did the Stevases not realize how hard she worked on this proposal? Hours of thought and effort down the drain. He arched a brow at his surrogate coordinator. *See? Never happy.*

"It's not that we don't like the idea," Linda said, at least having the good sense to sound apologetic. "I loved everything else."

"But Linda's lungs can't handle being around smoke. She'll end up coughing through the whole ceremony, and what kind of memory is that? This is supposed to be special."

Was the kid getting choked up? His eyes had a sheen to them.

Linda reached over and squeezed her husband's wrist. "It will be special," she said in a quiet voice. "But smokeless would be better."

"No problem," Larissa said before he could. "It's possible the shaman could purify the altar beforehand. Or..." She paused. "We can always do the ceremony without the shaman. Kind of a merger of traditional and nontraditional elements." Without missing a beat, she launched into a substitute idea. Carlos was doubly impressed. Smart and sexy. A dangerous combination. Her fiancé was a fool.

Without meaning to, his attention wandered to Larissa's legs. Her thighs were pale and smooth, like her shoulders last night. Linda had pale skin, too—most of the new arrivals did—but Larissa's skin had a creaminess to it that made it stand out amid all the bronze and copper. Her skin, her style of dress, her curves...everything about her stood out.

His late wife had been so breathtakingly beautiful. Perfect-looking, some said. Certainly, he thought so first time he laid eyes on her. Larissa Boyd wasn't nearly as flawless, but she had a radiance about her that pulled you in nonetheless. There was steel in there, too. Mirabelle had been so fragile, so unable to deal with a world that wasn't forever bright and shiny. Something told Carlos that Larissa Boyd created her own bright and shiny.

Was that the reason she held such appeal? Because she was so different from Mirabelle?

"And I'm sure the resort boutique can help you find a dress."

She was looking to him for a response. *"Si,"* he replied, after clearing his throat. "Señora Pedron, our shop manager, works closely with the boutiques in town. She will help you find whatever you need."

"I don't need anything super fancy," Linda said, "but I would like to wear something a little dressier than a cotton sundress. I would have packed more appropriately if someone told me about the ceremony in advance." She gave Paul a playful nudge, which he returned.

"I told you, I wanted to surprise you. Get whatever dress you want. Far as I'm concerned, you'd look gorgeous in a flour sack."

Naturally his answer made Linda beam. Poor besotted fool. Carlos mentally added up the costs. Paul Stevas's surprise was going cost a small fortune. With every expense agreed to while wearing a smile.

It was that damn smile that tried Carlos's nerves. His insipid adoring look cut too close to home. He'd worn a similar look those first months of his marriage, too. So willing to do anything to keep a smile on his wife's face. Too lost in his romantic haze to realize the impossibility of his job.

A few feet away, Larissa watched their banter with a rapture usually reserved for romantic movies. Carlos could only imagine the smile that would grace her face if he treated her to even a tiny slice of the gestures he bestowed on Mirabelle.

But then, a woman like Larissa would also expect feelings to go along with the gestures, wouldn't she? Feelings he couldn't give even in the shortest of terms. Mirabelle, with all her need, killed that possibility.

Still…he thought, his gaze sliding back to her legs. What he wouldn't do to feel the curve of her calf beneath his palm.

His view disappeared, destroyed by the re-crossing of legs in the opposite direction. "That's every detail I can think of," he heard Larissa say. "You're going to have a gorgeous recommitment ceremony."

"I'm sure we will," Paul said, kissing Linda again. "Thank you so much for all your help."

"I still can't believe I'm actually going to have my dream wedding. I probably won't sleep between now and Friday night."

"You better. I don't want you getting sick before we've said 'I do' again." Paul's comment earned him an eye roll. Such a sugary and adoring exchange, Carlos feared he might choke from the sweetness. To think he'd once sounded that way himself. Sipping his coffee, he offered silent thanks for intense Mexican brewing habits. The bitterness made for good balance. Like reality to fantasy.

"I'll have the catering office type up the notes and make sure a copy is left for you at the front desk," he told the Stevases. "If there are any questions or changes, please don't hesitate to ask."

"Should we call your office directly?" Paul asked. He'd directed his question at Larissa.

"I—uh—don't actually work here at the resort," Larissa replied, color creeping into her cheeks.

"You don't?" Linda's eyes were wider than usual. "You're certainly familiar with the services."

"Well, that's because—"

"Señorita Boyd is a good friend," Carlos said, jumping in. "The resort is between wedding coordinators at the moment, and she, being familiar with our services, graciously agreed to step in and help with your event."

"Ahhh." The newlyweds exchanged another look, and this time the knowing glance was easily decipherable. They mistook "friend" for something else.

"Then we appreciate your help even more," Linda told her.

"My pleasure," Larissa told her, shooting him a look of her own. She, too, had read what the Stevases were thinking. "If it's one thing I love, it's weddings, or pseudo-weddings in this case. I'm absolutely positive you're going to love what we've planned."

"You're coming to the ceremony right?"

"I make a point of stopping by every ceremony to make sure arrangements are to guests' liking," he told her.

"Yes, but will you and Larissa stay?"

She was asking if they would attend as a couple.

"I hadn't…" Larissa turned to him, and he shrugged, letting her know the decision was up to her. The woman had no reason to attend. This was her vacation; the Stevases were strangers. Curiously, his pulse quickened while he waited her response.

"Please," Linda said, grabbing Larissa's hand. "We've only a few family members coming in for the ceremony, and you've done so much to create this wonderful memory. It wouldn't feel right not having you there."

"Well, if it means so much to you—"

"Oh, it does! Thank you so much." Eyes filling with emotion, the young woman leapt from her chair and wrapped her arms around Larissa's neck. "For everything."

"Yes," Paul agreed. "You have no idea." His

eyes were damp, too. Clearly they were both prone to emotion as well as enamored with each other.

"Looks like I'll be attending a wedding this week after all," Larissa remarked once Paul and Linda departed. "Don't worry, I won't hold you to standing by my side."

The image of the two of them dancing on the beach flashed into his head. On their way to the elevator, Paul and Linda walked as though glued from shoulder to thigh. The thought of being glued in similar fashion while swaying to music sent his baser instincts into overdrive.

"You don't have to attend," he said, reaching for his coffee. "I could make an excuse. Tell them you aren't feeling well."

"No, I'd like to attend," she replied. "They seem like a sweet couple. They think we're dating, you know."

The remark caused him to cough into his coffee. "I assure you, that wasn't my intent when I first spoke. I was simply trying to avoid them knowing you were a guest."

"Why?"

The truth? He recognized Larissa's discomfort and felt compelled to rush in and save her embarrassment. There was no thought involved. "People expect more from a five-star resort than a guest covering a job in exchange for a discount on her bill," he replied. Perhaps not the entire answer, but truthful enough.

"I can see why you wouldn't want word to get out. Guests would crawl out of the woodwork looking for favors."

"Precisely." The shadow he thought he saw crossing her features had to be his imagination. "We are not in a position to be reducing bills left and right." No hotel was, and certainly not one who had their accounts mismanaged.

"However, I did not mean to make you feel uncomfortable," he added. "If you'd like, I will talk with them, and explain we are not together."

"You don't have to explain on my account. I mean—" she looked down "—it's only for one evening, and it's not like I'll see them again afterward. Besides, the two of them are so wrapped up in one another, I doubt they would remember the explanation anyway."

"Probably not." He ignored the surge that overtook him when Larissa said not to bother. Whether the Stevases' thought the two of them together was moot. They weren't. "Well, as you said, it is only for one evening."

"And there is no rule that says we have to spend the event together, because of a misconception, right?"

Was that expectancy in her voice? Carlos couldn't be sure, but all of a sudden her eyes reminded him of last night. So wide and blue. Kissing her would be a mistake. A very sweet-tasting mistake.

"*Si,*" he murmured. "There is not."

"Great." Larissa practically knocked the chair over jumping to her feet. Not her most graceful of moves, but then, she'd been stumbling mentally and physically the entire trip. "It looks like we're done here, so if you don't mind, seeing how I am a guest, I'm going to head back to my room."

"So quickly?" She couldn't blame him for being confused by her behavior. One moment, she's looking him in the eye, the next she was rushing to escape.

"There's a snorkeling trip to the ecopark leaving soon. If I hurry, I can join."

"I thought you didn't want to leave your lounge chair?"

"I wasn't, but snorkeling was on my original itinerary, and I realized last night there was no reason for me not to go through with my plans. I originally planned to go on Friday, but now that I've agreed to go to the recommitment ceremony, I need to pick a different day, so why not today?"

She smiled, hoping her smile didn't look nervous. Right before answering, Carlos's eyes had dropped to her mouth. While only a couple seconds ticked by, they'd lingered long enough to send some very disturbing thoughts into her head. First and foremost, the very clear realization that she wanted Carlos to kiss her, maybe more than she wanted him to last night.

Much as she hated to admit it, in slightly over twenty-four hours, she'd managed to develop a very serious fixation on the man. Tom, the man she should be thinking about, was barely a blip on the radar. She needed space and fresh air to clear her head.

If her departure disappointed Carlos, you couldn't tell from his expression. His eyes were as shuttered as always. "I won't keep you then. Enjoy your afternoon."

"Thanks, I will."

What did you think he'd say? Stay? The skin on the back of her neck prickled as she rushed her way to the elevator. If he was watching her departure, it was only because she acted so skittish. Anything more was kidding herself. Good thing she did decide to go snorkeling. A nice cool plunge in the tide pools was definitely what she needed to get a grip.

The launch back to her room took forever. Laid-back Mexican time did not work when you needed to stay distracted. Sitting in her seat only gave her more time to think. What did it say about her that she could be so drawn to a stranger on her honeymoon? Maybe she was as superficial as Tom said. She certainly hadn't given him a second thought while talking wedding details with Linda. If anything, she'd been excited that she would get to see her wedding ceremony take place after all. *She and Carlos.*

And with that thought the can of worms she'd fought so hard last night to ignore, ripped open to reveal the ugly truth: She didn't miss Tom at all. And if she didn't miss him, then he wasn't really her Prince Charming. She only thought he was because he wanted her, and being wanted was such a nice feeling.

Was that the reason she felt so attracted to Carlos? Because he looked at her with desire? That was so not a good reason.

CHAPTER SIX

IT WAS, HOWEVER, yet another reason to get away from the resort for a few hours. Soon as the launch reached her dock, Larissa rushed upstairs to her bedroom, pulling off her shirt as she ran. She had only a few minutes before the launch made its turn and passed by her dock. If she missed it, she'd have to either call another or rush back to the lobby by foot. Grabbing the first bathing suit she could find, a bright red one piece she normally hated because it emphasized her paleness, she tugged the spandex up over her hips while hopping around the room looking for the rest of her beach equipment. Why was it her sunscreen and sunglasses could never stay together?

Eventually, she located both, along with the snorkel equipment she'd brought with her. She clapped the fins together, to make sure there wasn't a tarantula hiding in a toehold, stuffed the equipment and a couple oversize beach towels into a tote and headed out the door.

A look out the glass-encased staircase told her she took too long to catch the launch, giving her no choice but to take the back way. This time of day, the sun was high and hot, not the kind of weather made for rushing. Fewer than five minutes into the dash, Larissa had sweat trickling down her back. Reminding herself she would be spending the afternoon in the water, she pushed on, making it back to the lobby in time to see the bus pull away from the curb.

Fantastic. Now she'd have to come up with another field trip to keep her mind distracted. Hot and sweaty, she sank to the curb to contemplate her options.

"We do have more comfortable places to sit," she heard a voice say. The deep timbre washed over her, setting off flutters in her stomach.

Glancing upward, she spotted Carlos standing by the valet stand, his presence obliterating everything around him.

"I missed the bus," she said lamely, as if he

couldn't guess by her woebegone appearance. "So I was trying to figure out what to do. I don't suppose there are taxis that go to Tulum?"

"There are always taxis. The question is how long it takes for them to arrive."

"Oh." It was beginning to sound like fate wanted her to stay on her lounge chair and think after all.

It dawned on her, that while she'd been rushing back and forth, her host had changed as well. Instead of his dark suit, he wore a pair of khaki shorts and a sport shirt, the white of which glowed against his copper-colored skin. Until this moment, Larissa had credited his black suit for his darkly sophisticated appearance. She'd been wrong. He looked sleeker than ever. "Are you going somewhere?"

"This afternoon is my afternoon off. I thought I'd take a drive off property." Looking for distraction and fresh air as well?

Just then, a battered black Jeep older than her pulled up to the curb she sat and a young man stepped out. "*Lo siento por el retraso,* Señor Chavez."

"*Gracias,* Hector."

This was Carlos's vehicle? Her amazement must have shown on her face, because he shot her an amused expression. "You look surprised."

"I am, a bit." Though she had no good reason except that based on his appearance, she'd expected something sexier. Not a mud-splattered car that looked like it fought in Normandy.

"Don't forget, we are in the jungle. When in Rome…"

Do as the Mayans do. Somehow, she didn't picture the Mayans having four-wheel drive. She could however, picture Carlos, with his jungle cat sleekness maneuvering around the jungle. Is that what he was off to do? Maneuver through the jungle? And why did the idea sound far more exotic when she included him?

She watched as he stashed a small cooler in the back before slipping a tip into the valet's hand. Right before he climbed into the driver's seat, he paused. "If you'd like, I could drive you."

Ride with him? In his car? The very man she was seeking space from? "Thank you, but that's not necessary."

"If you wait for a taxi, there's a good chance you'll waste your entire afternoon and I'd hate for a guest to miss out on an activity."

"I don't want to interfere with your plans."

"Since my plans are to take a drive, you aren't interfering with anything."

"I don't know..."

It was only a ride, right? Okay, granted the whole point of getting off site was so she could get away from his presence and think straight. On the other hand, if she continued arguing with him, she'd end up making a scene, and she didn't want that, either.

The driver behind him beeped his horn, the universe telling her to make up her mind and quick.

Carlos looked at her expectantly. "Larissa?"

"Why not?" Shouldering in her tote bag, she slipped into the passenger seat. It was only one ride.

As the Jeep bounced its way along the highway, Larissa did her best to keep her hat and sunglasses in place. Between the breeze and the

Jeep's aging shock absorbers, the job was harder than she thought it would be.

Out of the corner of her eye, she saw Carlos watching her. Even with sunglasses masking his stare, his attention still caused tingles to spread across her skin. Maybe this wasn't such a good idea after all. She tugged at her shorts, wishing she could make them magically lengthen and cover more of her thigh.

For some reason, the action made Carlos grin. "What?" she asked.

"Most people come to Mexico to expose their skin to the sun. You look like you're in disguise. I'm not helping you rob a bank, am I?"

Easy for him to joke. With his gorgeous skin, he wouldn't turn into a tomato in the sun. "You caught me. I'm really planning to rob the eco-park and have corralled you into driving my getaway car."

"I knew you weren't going for the tropical fish."

He had no idea how close his joke was to the truth.

A sign by the side of the road said they still had several kilometers before their exit. "Are you sure

I'm not disrupting your afternoon?" she asked again.

"I assure you, my plans are flexible. It's far more important that you be happy."

"Why?"

"Because you are a guest," he said, as though the answer were obvious.

He seemed to play the "guest" card often around her. Was it his not-so-subtle way of telling her not to read anything into his actions? Larissa wondered if her attraction was that blatantly obvious. Probably.

"Customer service is very important to you, isn't it?" she said. "I don't mean, simply because of recent events. It means a lot to you, what people think of your hotel."

"Because customers I can make happy."

"I don't understand." At first, she thought she heard wrong, he said the words so softly.

"*Lo siento.* I mean that, yes, how people view our resort is very important. The hotel's reputation is my reputation, and by extension, my family's. Discredit the hotel, discredit the Chavez name."

That wasn't what he said the first time, but she let the comment go. "My grandma used to say something similar, although it came out more like 'I won't have some high and mighty prom queen bitchin' all over town that I don't know how to sew.'"

"Your grandmother sounds like a very astute woman."

"She had her moments. I think when you're really good at your job, you can get away with being crotchety."

"And she was good?"

"Best in town. The house was always full of gowns. On the backs of closets, the china cabinet doors—basically anywhere she could hang a hook. Other kids had posters hung in their room. I had bridesmaid gowns."

"No wonder you became such an expert on weddings."

"If you can't beat 'em, join 'em, right? Do you know how hard it was, not to play dress up when I was little? All those beautiful gowns belonging to other people. My grandmother would have had a fit if I so much as breathed on one."

Remembering how badly she'd wanted to have a dress to call her own, she felt a hollow feeling spread across her chest. *Careful. That's how you got in this mess. By wanting to belong.*

"My brother Pedro dressed up in one of our mother's gowns once. My brothers and I never let him forget how pretty he looked."

Larissa smiled, both at the image and his attempt to lighten the mood. "Sounds like Delilah and me when our friend Chloe dyed her hair. We still tease her about looking like a wire-haired circus clown."

"Your friends…the three of you sound very close."

"I don't know what I'd do without them. They're the closest thing I have to a family these—" Damn. It'd be too much to hope he didn't catch her slip, wouldn't it?

"I didn't realize your grandmother had passed. I'm sorry."

No, she was the one who was sorry, because the whole story was more pathetic. "We'd stopped talking long before, so it wasn't a huge loss."

"I'm sorry. Did you have a fight?"

"Not really. Once I turned eighteen, she um… well, she sort of retired."

"From dressmaking."

"From raising me." She cringed knowing what he must be thinking. A man like him from a large, established family. "It's not as bad as it sounds. After all, I'd left Texas behind, so why shouldn't she leave me? After all, she'd already had to raise two generations on her own." Wasn't her grandmother's fault time had wrung out the best of her.

"What about the rest of your family?"

Ah, that. She should have realized that she couldn't mention a second generation without getting a question or two. "There isn't any more. At least any that I care to talk to." If her mother, wherever she was these days, wanted to find her, she would have. Wasn't like she was hiding out.

Carlos reached over and covered her hand with his. "I am sorry if I brought up a sad topic."

"You didn't." She watched as his thumb made small circles on the back of her hand. His touch chased the hollow feeling away. If only she could entwine their fingers and hold on tight.

To her dismay, he moved his hand back to the steering wheel. "Why don't we make a pledge, to focus on pleasant topics for the rest of the ride?" he suggested. "Are you looking forward to snorkeling at the ecopark?"

"Both will be new experiences," she replied. "Have you been? To the ecopark, that is."

"I have. It's very nice. Crowded though. Most of the serious divers prefer more out-of-the-way places." He paused, and Larissa could see an idea forming in his head. "Would you be interested in trying a different location? One that wasn't so touristy?"

"Sure. Why not? I'm not all that keen on crowds myself. Where do you suggest I go?"

His profile broke in to a slow smile. Damn if the look didn't make her nerves tingle with excitement. "You willing to trust me?"

A loaded question to be sure. In spite the warnings whispering in her ear, Larissa shrugged. "Sure. Why not?"

It was only snorkling. Sitting back, Larissa watched the road signs for clues to their destination, seeing none. A short time later, they turned off the highway onto a narrow unmarked road which in turn became dirt. The narrow pathway was carved with ruts and potholes so deep she feared one might swallow them up. Tropical foliage formed a wall on either side of them, the broad leaves reaching out to slap the sides of the Jeep. Forgetting about trying to save her hat, she reached up to grab the roll bar to save herself.

"You won't fall out, if that's what you're worried about," Carlos said.

Maybe not, but holding on made her feel more secure. "What kind of road is this, anyway?"

"I believe Americans would call it the road less traveled."

Did the road get traveled at all? They hit another pothole and she gripped the bar tighter. Now she understood the point of driving the Jeep, as well as what happened to the shocks. "Is it going to be this bouncy the entire way?" She might not fall out, but another jolt like that one, and she'd need her spine realigned.

"We're almost there," he said. Ahead, nailed to trunk of a large tree was a wooden sign on which someone had painted...something. The letters were too faded to read clearly, although Larissa thought she made out the letters *C, N* and *T.* A few feet beyond, the road narrowed even further, becoming no more than a rocky foot path that ended with a rusty gate held shut by a chain.

The first thing that struck her when he cut the engine, was the quiet. There wasn't a sound beyond the rustle of leaves and the occasional caw of a bird. Carlos got out and walked to the rear where he removed her beach bag and his cooler. "We will have to go the rest of the way by foot," he told her. "It's not a very far walk. No more than a quarter mile."

Question was, a walk to where? All of a sudden she wasn't so certain about this trip. *Serves you right,* she said to herself, as a giant mosquito buzzed her ear. A warm, earthy smell hung in the air. Without the breeze, her skin was already hot and sticky. She took a step, only to turn her ankle on a rock.

"Careful! The path is uneven." In a flash, Carlos appeared at her elbow and despite carrying their belongings, still managed to have a hand free to guide her. Larissa did her best not to shiver as his fingers brushed her bare skin.

"Is it safe to leave the Jeep parked here like this?" she asked. Every piece of literature she read cautioned about leaving belongings unattended, yet here they were parking an open car in the middle of the jungle. She was suddenly having visions of being stranded. Not because she didn't trust her companion—if anything, she trusted him too much—but with the way her luck had been running this week, who knew what could happen.

"The Jeep will be fine. Pablo will keep an eye on it."

"Pablo?"

He pointed to where the path turned into a clump of foliage. Beyond the bushes, the path split into two, one way continuing on into the trees, the other leading uphill to a small building.

She waited while Carlos rattled the chain against the gate. *"Hola!"* he greeted. *"Estamos aquí para nadir en el cenote!"*

"There's a *cenote* here?" Hearing the word, Larissa suddenly realized that's what was painted on the sign. She craned her neck hoping to spot one of the famous Yucatán underwater sinkholes but saw nothing but dirt and scrub.

"The landowner discovered it on his property several years ago. Mostly locals use it, but the resort sends divers here when they are looking for someplace off the beaten path."

A thin gray-haired man ambled out of the building and down the path. *"Cincuenta pesos cada uno. Y no proporcionamos chalecos salvavidas."*

Carlos turned to her. "How's your swimming?"

"Pretty good," she replied. Enough so she could hold her own in deep water.

"No problema."

Larissa tried to keep up with the exchange, but her Spanish was too rusty and basic to understand most of what was being said. Based on the fact Carlos reached into his pocket and peeled off several bills, she assumed the man was the aforementioned Pablo. The old man stuffed the money in his pocket, then wordlessly opened the gate. *"Asquirese de tomar su basura,"* he said as he let them pass.

"He's really got his people skills down," she noted after the man headed back to his house.

"Now you know why only the locals visit. I think Pablo considers visitors a necessary evil. If he didn't like the money, he'd keep everyone off his property. The *cenote* is this way." He gestured toward the path on the right, leading into the jungle.

Larissa picked her way beside him, keeping an eye on the ground so she wouldn't stumble again. Stumbling meant Carlos would reach out and catch her. The way she reacted to his touch disturbed her. Tom touched her hundreds of times, and far more intimately at that, and she never broke out in shivers.

"Do you come here a lot?" Until today, she wouldn't have said he looked like the swimming hole kind of guy, although she had to admit, the shorts made him look like a different person.

"Once, when I first arrived, so I knew the kind of place the front desk clerks were recommending. I didn't want to be blindsided by a bad review."

Why wasn't she surprised? Guests seemed to be the most important part of his world.

Dear Lord, but it was hot. For something that was supposed to protect her from the sun, her hat wasn't doing a very good job. The back of her neck felt like it was on fire. "Do we have much further?"

"We're here."

Looking up, Larissa saw the vegetation had dropped away, creating a large cavern in the middle of the trees. Peering over the edge, she saw a pool a hundred or so feet below, part of the great underground river system that flowed beneath the entire Yucatán peninsula. The water was so clear, that despite the drop, she could make out rock formations in its depths.

"You're right," she said, smiling up at Carlos. "This is way better than the ecopark." Better than better; they had the entire place to themselves.

A crude wooden ladder lead into the cavern. With Carlos leading the way, they climbed to the base. There the rocks formed a natural spiral staircase leading to the water.

"I can see why the Mayans thought these places

were portals to the underworld," Larissa remarked. It really was like entering another world.
Tree roots twisted from above like giant gnarled
fingers, their ends disappearing into the rocks
beneath the water. Meanwhile, long strings of
vegetation formed a curtain along one edge. Sunlight streamed through the gaps to fill the dark
space with an otherworldly glow. Nature's mood
lighting.

"Be careful," Carlos said. "The condensation
makes the rocks slippery and unless you want to
practice your cliff diving, I'd watch your step."

Larissa took the warning to heart and pressed
a palm to the wall. After a few more minutes,
they reached bottom. The rock formed a shelf a
few inches above the water. Beneath the surface,
Larissa caught sight of a school of fish darting
away from one of the stalagmites and gasped
with delight.

"This is amazing! I can't believe we have the
whole place to ourselves."

"I did see snorkeling equipment poking out of
that bag of yours, right?"

"You did." The water was so clear she could

see the stalagmites rising up from the depths. She couldn't wait to jump in and explore. Ditching her hat and sunglasses, she reached for the hem of her T-shirt. No sooner did she start to lift the garment than she froze. Carlos was in the process of peeling off his shirt, and damn if he didn't make the task look effortless. The cotton slipped up and over his head in one swift movement. He'd definitely been a cat in a previous life. His body was sleek, with muscles made for action, not show. A dusting of dark hair lent an unnecessary rugged edge.

"If it's all right, I thought I'd cool off while you explored," he said, when he caught her watching. "Is that a problem?"

"Don't be silly. Of course it's not a problem." Beyond the fact he was standing shirtless while she was about to strip off her clothes. *Dear Lord, she'd pressed her hand against that chest.* She raised her own shirt, conscious of every wiggle and twist needed to pull the garment over her head. The air hit her bare shoulders in a rush, causing goose bumps. At that moment, her one-piece bathing suit felt way too skimpy. When she finally pulled her head free, she found their positions reversed, and Carlos was staring at her.

"Be careful," he said. Was it her imagination or has voice dropped a notch? "The water's very deep."

"O-okay." Her mouth suddenly dry, she swallowed, then reached for her waistband. Carlos eyes locked with hers. Without breaking their gaze, she popped the button on her shorts and slipped them over her hips. They dropped to the rock with barely a sound. They stood inches apart, the sound of their breathing magnified by the close space, making it seem as though no other noise existed.

Larissa had never felt more exposed. The whole moment was fraught with an intimacy way beyond their surroundings. As for Carlos, his eyes still hadn't released their hold on hers. In the dim light, they looked darker than ever. Predatory, even. She wished she could see past their surface to know what he was thinking, but like all the other times he'd looked at her, she found their depths shuttered.

That didn't stop her skin from igniting from

the inside out. Or an ache from starting low in her stomach. She felt on the edge of a far bigger plunge than the water beside her.

"Who dives in first?" Her voice came out a whisper, the question's double meaning hanging in the air.

A strand of hair clung to her damp cheek. She shivered as Carlos brushed it away. *"Dios me ayude,"* he whispered in return. Then, turning, he dove in to the clear blue water.

Good idea, thought Larissa, ignoring the heavy disappointment in her stomach. *Take the safe plunge.*

CHAPTER SEVEN

"Surely, you are a prune by now?"

Rotating onto her back, Larissa pushed off the ledge with her feet, the water slapping the rock with a soft whoosh. "Possibly," she replied. "I didn't check."

Okay, she had checked, but she wasn't ready to dry off. So long as she stayed in the water, she could avoid dealing with what happened earlier. The tension between them seemed to grow stronger with each passing moment. At some point, the line had to snap, sending them in one direction or another. Her body knew what direction it wanted. Forty minutes in the cool water and it still tingled from his touch.

And, he'd merely brushed his fingers across her skin. Goodness knows how her body would feel if he actually kissed her. Her mind, on the other hand, wasn't entirely sure finding out was a good idea.

Which was why, pruny fingers be damned, she stayed in the water while Carlos lounged on the rock shelf like a copper-skinned god.

"You have to remember," she told him, "we don't have underground rivers and caves in New York. We have sewers."

"Mexico isn't all *cenote*s and tropical lagoons, either, you know. We have our droughts, our poor sewage systems, our earthquakes—"

"Yeah, yeah. Stop being a buzzkill."

"I'm simply trying to inject a little reality and remind you no place is perfect."

Maybe not, but her current location certainly came close.

Using the backstroke, she glided across the surface and stared at the cloudless blue sky through the chamber opening. "I still can't believe I'm swimming in my own private underground cave," she said. Her favorite part was on the far side of the cavern. There, above two giant root systems, the water flowed from the source in a waterfall. She angled her body in that direction, prattling as she paddled.

"When I was a kid, I watched this movie about star-crossed island lovers. In it, the hero comes across the heroine bathing in a lagoon. I remember thinking how she rinsed her hair in the waterfall was the coolest thing ever."

"Should I go ask Pablo for some shampoo?"

"Would you?" She leaned back and let the stream wash off her forehead. Somehow she suspected the host in him would oblige if he thought her serious. "Anyway, the princess falls in love with the hero. Or Bob Hope. I don't remember which one."

"Sounds like you watched a lot of movies."

"Tons. My grandmother used to sew to the classic movie channel." And God forbid she should change the channel. "While other kids grew up with video games, I grew up counting satin buttons and watching Errol Flynn rescue princesses."

"I'm beginning to see where you got your romantic streak."

"What can I say? I'm a sucker for happy endings."

"Except life isn't like the movies, is it?" A soft plop echoed through the chamber. It was Carlos tossing a pebble into the water. He sat leaning forward with his body hunched over his knees, his attention focused somewhere in the depths.

"That doesn't mean happy endings don't happen."

"Don't tell me you still believe happy endings are possible after what happened with your own engagement?"

"Why shouldn't I?" She had to believe in them. Otherwise, the alternative was that she didn't get a happy ending, and that idea was untenable. Surely after sitting on the sidelines for so long, she deserved some happiness, even if she failed this time around. "Look at Paul and Linda. They're happy."

"Si," he replied. His unspoken *for now* hung in the air.

The waterfall's appeal faded. Turning around, she began the slow kick back toward the ledge. "My friend Delilah has this saying," she told him.

"Every puzzle has its missing piece, and I think she's right."

"I don't understand."

"It means all of us have that one special person who completes us. Our soul mate."

Carlos laughed and took a drink from the water bottle he'd retrieved from his cooler. "If that were true, La Joya wouldn't have repeat customers."

"I'm serious."

"So am I. Five years from now, at least a third of the people lounging by the hotel pool will be unhappy. What will you say about soul mates then?"

"I'll point out the two-thirds who *are* happy, that's what." Why was he so determined to rain on her parade? "I have to admit, I really don't understand why you're so cynical. You were married."

"An experience that taught me quite definitively that nothing lasts forever."

He tried to sound casual, but pain still leaked from between the words. How deep his grief must run. The thought left an ache beneath her breastbone. Was that why he closed off his gaze?

Was he trying to keep the world from seeing how much he hurt?

"I'm sorry," she said in a soft voice.

Carlos set down the bottle. His eyes were black as he looked down into the water. "For what?"

For the fact he'd been left alone. For his anger. "You must have loved your wife very much."

"Why do you say that?"

"Why else would you be so angry?"

She watched as his attention moved to an invisible spot on the rock. His finger scratched at the surface, each stroke leaving a wet streak, black against gray. "I fell in love with my wife the moment I laid eyes on her. I would have done anything for her."

And she died leaving him alone. Larissa still didn't understand the cynicism, but she did get the bitterness.

He reached down to grab her by the hand. "Your lips are turning blue. Come out and towel off."

"My lips are not blue," Larissa protested. She grabbed his hand anyway, marveling at how effortlessly he pulled her up. Once out of the water, the cold air hit her skin and the comfortable body temperature she'd been enjoying disappeared into a fit of shivers. Instantly, a fluffy towel settled around her shoulders. "See?" Carlos said. "Blue."

He tightened the terrycloth cocoon, then brushed the damp hair from her face. The sensation of his fingers caressing her skin ignited a new set of shivers.

"You must miss her very much."

"I miss— She shouldn't have died."

"No, she shouldn't have," Larissa replied. What were the words he bit back? Did he think she wouldn't notice the sorrow in his words? The man could shutter his expression all he wanted, but clearly, he hurt and hurt deeply. With good reason. The love of his life died too young. Still, something about the way held back made her think there was more to the story.

"You stayed in too long, *querida*," he told her.

"Did I?" Based on how her insides were trembling, she wondered if she should still be swimming.

"*Si.* You need to be careful. Too long, and you'll grow weak from the cold."

"I'm not cold."

"Your shivering says otherwise."

Larissa looked him in the eye, her gaze telling him what they both already knew: that her trembling had nothing to do with the water. His hands slowed, the touch becoming sensual. "I don't…I'm not…" He struggled for words to caution her no doubt but the way his gaze dropped to her mouth even as he spoke left no doubt as to what he wanted.

"Me, neither," Larissa whispered. This was purely physical. Two people giving into an attraction and nothing more. That her heart pounded in her chest in anticipation meant nothing.

Carlos cupped her jaw. *"Tan bella,"* he murmured. *"Me vuelves loco."*

She wanted to ask the translation, but his mouth slanted over hers, erasing all thoughts of conversation. He kissed like he moved, confident and masterful, his lips coaxing a response without effort. Her eyes fluttered shut. Tom's kisses never felt like this. Carlos's kiss pulled the ground out from her feet. It made her head spin. She was dizzy, breathless, aching for more.

And then it ended, broken by a need for air. Carlos's breath was ragged as he rested his forehead against hers. A solitary Spanish oath escaped his lips. Larissa didn't need to translate the hoarsely whispered word. She felt the same way. Just what that feeling was, she couldn't say for sure, but all of a sudden, to call their attraction *purely physical,* sounded very inadequate.

"We should go," Carlos said, breaking away.

"You want to leave?"

This disappointment in her voice killed him, and it was all he could do to rein in his impulse to erase the tone from her voice. Of course he didn't want to leave. He wanted to pull her back into his arms and kiss her senseless. But with his head spinning, going back to La Joya was the better option. He turned so he wouldn't have to look her in the eye. Any kind of sad expression would be the death of him. "The evening shift starts soon. I need to go back in case there are questions."

"What's the matter, afraid the hotel won't manage without you?"

He could sense her smile. "You sound like

Jorge. He tells me the same thing, although this is the longest I've stayed away since our arrival. I'm curious to see how he reacts." Originally, he planned only on taking a drive to clear his head, ironically enough, of his thoughts about her.

"I'm sorry if I screwed up your afternoon."

"Don't be silly. I'm the one who offered." He was still trying to figure out what made him make the suggestion in the first place instead of driving her to the ecopark as planned. One moment she'd been talking about her childhood, fighting hard to keep her voice upbeat and positive while telling a story that was anything but, the next he was possessed with the urge to show her something unique gripped him.

To make her smile...

So what if he did want to do something nice? Larissa did him a great service today. Why not treat her to something out of the ordinary. His decision had nothing to do with how her story squeezed at the center of his chest. Nothing whatsoever.

As for the kiss... What could he do? She'd been stirring his blood from the moment she opened her hotel room door, and there was only so much resistance a man could muster, especially a man who'd been living as a monk for half a decade.

A soft sigh broke his thoughts. Turning, he saw Larissa folding her towel, a wistful expression on her face. She caught him looking, and blushed. His chest squeezed again.

"I know I've said it before, but thank you for an amazing afternoon," she said. "This place is unlike anything I could have imagined."

"I'm glad. Considering how helpful you were with the Stevases, showing you an underground river is the least I can do."

"Anything to make a guest happy, right?"

"Naturally." No sooner did he speak than he regretted his answer. "I didn't mean—"

"Relax. I was making a joke."

Then why did her eyes turn shadowy? Perhaps the fading light was playing tricks with his head. Too many years of weighing every sentence lest he say the wrong thing had turned him overly wary. If Larissa said she was joking, he should take her for her word.

"You're more than a regular guest," he told her.

"I should think so, unless you kiss all your guests."

"No. You're the exception."

"Good to know."

With his confession came a bout of nerves, bubbling up from place he couldn't name. He needed to explain his actions fully. So she would understand. "It wasn't planned," he rushed to explain. "The kiss, that is. I'm not…" Again the words failed him. How did you explain to a woman who talked of island princesses and soul mates that the woman you thought was the love of your life drained you dry?

She rallied a smile, saving him. "There's no need to explain. I understand."

"You do?" Because he wasn't sure he did anymore.

"Sure. Sometimes a kiss is just a kiss."

Carlos let out a silent sigh. "*Gracias, querida.* I'm glad we are on the same page."

Although he'd feel better if she hadn't quoted another movie.

Or if a tiny voice in the back of his brain didn't disagree.

* * *

It didn't take long for them to pack their belongings and climb back to the surface. When they reached the top of the ledge steps, Larissa paused to snap a photo with her cell phone. Something to help her remember paradise. On a whim, she snapped a photo of Carlos as well, catching his profile as he looked down at the water. Another memory to hold.

She lied when she told him a kiss was just a kiss. Kissing Carlos was more like a carnival thrill ride: Exhilarating, euphoric, a dizzying freefall that left her insides trembling with adrenaline and eager to ride again. Would she, though, or was his kiss, like this afternoon's surprise trip, a one-time deal?

Above ground, the weather was as hot as the *cenote* had been cool. By the time they walked back to the entrance and waited for Pablo to unlock the gate, Larissa had gone from refreshed to sweaty again. Perspiration ran down her back and between her breasts.

"So much for blue lips," she said, pulling at the

ruching on her swimsuit. "I have half a mind to turn around and head back to the cavern."

"I'm—"

Again, she rushed to reassure him. She appeared to be doing that a lot this afternoon; reassuring saved her from hearing apologies. "Evening staff meeting, I know."

They walked into the lobby to find a scowling Jorge pacing behind the front desk. "Don't you answer your phone?" he snapped.

"We were in the jungle. You know what the reception is like. What's the problem?"

"We?" His eyes switched to Larissa, and his expression softened. "Oh. I didn't realize. *Lo siento,* Señorita Boyd. I've been trying to contact my cousin regarding an issue that requires his attention."

Carlos shot her a look that said *See?* "What is the problem?"

Jorge learned close and spoke in low, rapid Spanish.

Larissa caught the words right before Carlos grimaced.

"I'm going to have to handle this right away," he said, his eyes apologetic. "Do you mind taking the launch back on your own?"

She smiled so he wouldn't see her disappointment. Foolish, but she'd hoped…

She didn't know what she hoped. That goodbye might be more? Summoning a bright smile, she pretended the dismissal didn't sting. "Of course not. I've already taken up way too much of your time as it is. I'm sure there are many guests that need your attention now."

It took some effort, but she managed to slip her bag from his grip without brushing his fingers. "Thank you for a fantastic afternoon, Señor Chavez. I appreciate your attention."

She turned away before he could respond.

Later, as she sat on her terrace nursing another twenty-dollar cola, she wondered if she reacted too dramatically. After all, Carlos had done his best to be honest. Any unspoken words were because she cut him off. Maybe the kiss didn't have the same effect on him. It was entirely possible her reaction had more to do with his skill than any kind of connection.

What she should be pondering was how easily Tom had slipped from her mind. Six weeks ago, she'd been prepared to walk down the aisle and now here she was, kissing another man. Were her feelings for her ex so anemic they could be displaced that easily?

As far as comparisons went, the two men were like night and day. Carlos might look sleek and confident, but beneath the surface lay a sadness she'd yet to fully measure. One moment he made her pulse race; the next she wanted to hold him in her arms and tell him everything would be all right.

On the other hand Tom…Tom wanted to marry her. Oh, sure, he was a nice guy—intelligent, kind and successful—but mainly, he wanted her, and Larissa considered herself darn lucky to be wanted. Not once, though, did his kisses leave her insides trembling the way today's kiss did. At best, his kisses were like the man himself: nice.

She sighed. Much as she hated to admit, Tom did her a favor breaking the engagement. The two of them were far from soul mates. Carlos's kiss proved as much.

Listen to yourself. Sitting here acting like kissing Carlos was more than a bit of rebound entertainment. Larissa shook her head. Who knows what Carlos was to her? She didn't even know if she'd see him again the rest of the trip. His kiss, however… His kiss would stay with her a long, long time.

On the other side the lagoon, the egrets had begun bedding down for the evening. Pairs and trios swooped into the foliage, their feathers dotting the canopy white. They called out to each other, other birds joining in until the entire lagoon was alive with squawking. Her own personal nighttime serenade, Larissa thought with a sleepy smile. Swimming had taken more out of her than she thought, and she could feel her eyes growing heavy. Closing them, she let the birds' song float her away. Carlos was wrong. Flaws or not, Mexico was paradise. If she could, Larissa would never leave.

Seemed like only seconds later when she opened her eyes to dark gray and quiet. Falling asleep on the divan was becoming way too easy. Yawning, she padded her way inside to the darkening living room. From the look out her oceanside window, the sun had only recently set. Red and orange closed on the horizon line, the colors making a bright line between the black water and gray sky.

As if answering a call only it could hear, her attention moved to the walkway and the figure standing below her window. Larissa's pulse quickened. *Carlos.* He stood in the shadows, but it didn't matter; she knew what he wanted. She walked downstairs and opened the door.

"Hey," she greeted, her voice barely audible over the surf. "Crisis averted?"

"A guest thought someone stole some jewelry. Turns out she simply misplaced the items."

"So, there was a happy ending after all."

Carlos smile flashed white in the darkening sky. "For now."

He wasn't going to give an inch on the issue, was he? At the moment, Larissa wasn't in the mood to argue the point. Soon as she saw him, a twisting longing had begun spiraling through her erasing any and all of the very logical self-arguments she'd given herself earlier. "That mean your duties are done for the evening?"

"I don't know," he replied. "Are they?"

Smiling, Larissa opened the door wider and let him inside.

"Mind if I join you?"

The sight of Linda Stevas holding a plate of scrambled eggs and fruit wasn't what Larissa hoped to see when she decided to take coffee on the terrace. She'd been scanning the walkway below for a familiar black suit, hoping to catch Carlos on his morning property check. To ask him how he slept, she thought, smiling to herself.

There were times when she thought the past two nights were dreams. Her body remembered, however. Granted, she didn't have a long list of lovers for comparison, but being with Carlos made her feel alive in a way she didn't know was possible. Like his kisses, his lovemaking left her breathless and unsteady. She couldn't get enough. Neither could he. Both nights passed in a haze of lovemaking and pillow talk that lasted until gray seeped through the cracks in the mangroves, and

Larissa couldn't keep her eyes open any longer. Then morning would arrive, and she'd wake up alone, the only sign she'd had company the rumpled sheets and love bites marking the back of her shoulder. She thought of asking him to stay, but fearing his answer, decided to accept what he could give.

It was, she told herself, a vacation fling in its truest form. Hadn't both she and Carlos assured one another neither was looking for more?

Why, then, did she have this nagging feeling the rules had changed, at least where she was concerned? With each kiss, each whispered word of intimacy, she found herself hoping this would be the time she looked in Carlos's eyes and found their depths no longer shuttered.

"Larissa?" Linda looked at her expectantly. "I'm not disturbing you, am I?"

"Not at all." Swallowing her disappointment, Larissa smiled and gestured for the woman to take a seat.

"Are you sure? I thought maybe you were waiting for Señor Chavez."

Truer words… "Carlos is working. I'll see him

later." She tried to contain the thrill the thought gave her, and failed. "Speaking of eating companions, however, where's your other half?" She thought the couple inseparable.

"I convinced him to take a run on the beach. We spent yesterday at the local hospital, and he's a little stressed out from the experience."

"The hospital? Is everything okay? It wasn't anything serious, was it?"

"I was having some trouble catching my breath, but everything's fine now. No big deal."

Was it really no big deal? While the young woman certainly looked fine, the way she suddenly focused on her plate made Larissa wonder. It would be a shame if, after so much effort, Linda got sick and couldn't enjoy her recommitment ceremony. It would explain why the young woman was downplaying yesterday's emergency.

"Anyway," she said, taking a bite of pineapple, "I figured he should mellow out a little before our parents arrive."

"You must be getting excited."

"You have no idea." The woman's eyes sparkled. "I found the perfect dress while in town yesterday. White with flowers hand-stitched around the neckline. It fits, too. I was so afraid I'd end up looking like I was wearing an over-size sack."

Larissa understood. Growing up, she'd heard customers uttering the same lament too many times to count, and given Linda's obscenely thin figure, she could imagine the challenge.

"I feel a little bad about how much it cost," Linda was saying, "but Paul told me not to worry."

"Listen to your husband. He clearly wants you to be happy."

"Yeah, Paul's great that way. He keeps telling me he wants me to have the wedding of my dreams this time around. I'm so lucky to have him," she said, eyes growing damp.

The Stevases' devotion to one another was enviable. Too bad Carlos wasn't here to see the love on Linda's face. Maybe it might change his cynical view to see two happy people.

"I bet if I ask, he'll say he's lucky to have you, as well."

"I hope so. I hated to think he's doing all this

simply out of... Never mind." The young woman shook off whatever she was about to say. "Tomorrow is going to be absolutely perfect. You're still coming, right?"

"Absolutely. I wouldn't miss it for the world. I'm kind of excited to see what the shaman will do." After a bit of negotiation, Carlos convinced the man to compromise on his cleansing ritual, enabling the Stevas› to have the full traditional ceremony. And the man claimed he wasn't romantic.

"Me, too," Linda replied. She started to take a bite of food, only to drop the fork and rush to the other side of the table. "I'm sorry," she said, pulling Larissa into a hug. "I'm so happy, I can't help myself. You and Señor Chavez have no idea how much this ceremony means to both Paul and me."

"No, but I think I can guess," Larissa said, patting her back. Hard not to want to help the couple, what with the way they seemed so in love.

"I hope I'm not interrupting a female bonding session?"

Carlos? Larissa entangled herself from the embrace to see him striding toward their table.

His black suit crisp as ever, his hair perfectly in place, he looked nothing like the lover who kept her up all night. That is, until his eyes dropped to her lips, and the flash of familiar possessive hunger she saw sent heat curling around the base of her spine.

He might as well have kissed her consider the onslaught of shyness attacking her. Tucking her hair behind her ear, she turned away with a smile. "I thought you made your morning rounds this hour."

"Actually I was on my way to call Señora Stevas's room when I spotted her on the terrace."

"You were looking for me?"

Larissa's heart started to sink, and she kicked herself. She had absolutely no reason to feel disappointed. Did she think he was the only guest at the resort Carlos thought about?

No, just the only one he was sleeping with.

"I wanted to let you know we were able to book a moonlight lagoon cruise for you and your husband Friday night."

"Really?"

"Yes. And I've directed the launch driver to

take you to the outmost point of the lagoon so your anniversary can be celebrated in private. The chef will call you later today regarding the menu."

"Oh, my gosh, I'm so excited. I'm going up to the room and see if Paul's back from his run. He's going to be so excited." Jumping up from the table, the young woman drew Carlos into a hug, which, Larissa noted with a smile, he awkwardly returned.

"She's very...exuberant," he remarked after Linda had bustled off.

"Can you blame her?" Larissa asked. "You know, for a man who claims to detest romance, you went out of your way to create a very romantic evening. Directing the launch operator to sail to a remote location?"

"We direct all the operators to sail to remote locations," he replied, taking the seat Linda vacated. "Telling the guests lets them feel special. Those special touches are what lead to good reviews."

And goodness knows reviews were important

to him. "Well, I'm sure Paul and Linda will sing the resort's praises to everyone under the sun."

"Let us hope so."

Judging from Linda's enthusiasm, Larissa was pretty sure she could guarantee it. She smiled over the rim of her coffee. "You look tired this morning." Dark smudges marked his bronze skin.

"I'm afraid I didn't get much sleep last night. Seems there was a rather high-maintenance guest who required my attention."

"Is that so? What a shame. Perhaps she'll be less demanding tonight so you can sleep."

A gleam appeared in his eye. "I certainly hope not. Her 'demands' have been the best part of my week."

Larissa flushed from head to toe. He'd purposely dropped his voice to a husky timbre, making her mouth run dry. "Then she'll definitely demand more."

"Good." The air stilled around them. Feeling bold, Larissa slid her leg forward until the inside of her sandal pressed against his wingtip. To anyone walking by, the position looked benign, but for them, the touch held unspoken promise. To Larissa's pleasure, Carlos actually smiled.

"Señora Stevas wasn't the only person I was heading to see," he said.

"Really?" Her stomach gave another one of those flutters. "Did you want something?"

"It appears one of our guests canceled their dinner cruise reservation for this evening. I was wondering if you would be interested in joining me."

"You want to take me on a moonlight cruise?"

He shrugged, as though the offer was no big deal. "I remembered you mentioning to the Stevases how much you'd been looking forward to going, and how disappointed you were to have to cancel your own. I thought I'd offer you the opportunity to indulge in another one of your itinerary items. But if you don't wish to—"

"I didn't say I wasn't interested."

Next to the wedding ceremony, the moonlight lagoon cruise had been the one item she'd most looked forward to. So much so, she actually contemplated having the dinner by herself. Having dinner with Carlos, however, sounded much more inviting.

He arched his brow. "But?"

"But…" She paused, wondering how to phrase her question. Going on a dinner cruise, was very much like a public date. "Your staff will see us together."

"You have a problem with them seeing us together?"

"I don't." But a man who made a point of high-tailing it from her room at dawn might. "I assumed when it came to your personal life, you preferred to maintain a low profile around your staff."

"You forget, *querida,*" he said, leaning forward. "My staff knows how to be discreet. So are you interested?"

"Very."

"Good. The launch will be in front of your dock at seven o'clock."

Just in time to enjoy the sunset. If she said something, he'd probably tell her the boats always departed at sunset to increase the ambiance. She preferred not to know. "I'll be there."

"So will I." He reached over and ran a finger along the inside of her wrist, trumping her foot move by spades. "'Til tonight, *querida*."

Watching him walk away, Larissa rubbed the spot on her skin where his finger made contact, and tried not to think about how he completely dodged her comment about being public.

CHAPTER EIGHT

"Hola, chica! Que pasa?"

Chloe's voice burst over the receiver. Hearing her friend caused a ripple of homesickness. Back home, they barely went a day without chatting. "Just having breakfast overlooking the ocean," Larissa replied. After Carlos went back to his office, she remained, using the view to distract her from thinking too hard. "What about you? Aren't you supposed to be working? Or have you finally decided to quit and help your boyfriend run his coffee empire?"

"Nah, I'm saving those kinds of life-changing decisions for when you get back."

"We're on speakerphone in Simon's office," a second voice, Delilah's, chimed in. "We told him we needed to check on you. We were worried because you didn't return our phone call the other day."

She'd completely forgotten they called while she was getting sick. "I'm so sorry, you guys, I meant to."

"Relax," Chole replied. "We're only teasing. We didn't expect you to call back. International cell calls are expensive."

"Plus, you should be out enjoying your vacation," Delilah added. "How is Mexico?"

"Wonderful, now that I've recovered from your welcome present. I'm never drinking champagne again. Oh, and then there was the tarantula." Briefly, she told them about her encounter with Hairy.

True to form, Delilah expressed the proper sympathy, while Chloe giggled. "Poor La-Roo," she said. "So far paradise hasn't been very nice to you."

"It hasn't been all bad." In fact, she added silently as Carlos's midnight smile flashed before her, some of Mexico had been very, very good. "I went swimming in an underground cave the other day. And, tonight I'm taking a moonlight cruise on the lagoon."

"How lovely," Delilah said, only to pause

shortly after. "Wait, I thought those lagoon cruises were a private, couples-only thing. Who are you going with? Don't tell me you're taking one by yourself."

Larissa bit her lip. Should she tell them about Carlos? Normally, the three of them shared everything, but she didn't feel like talking about her time with Carlos. Not yet anyway. She was having a hard enough time examining the circumstances in the harsh light of day; talking would only expose the flaws and bring her bubble closer to bursting.

Unfortunately, in a huge tactical error, she forgot how her friends could read between the lines, especially the lines of a prolonged silence.

"Something's up," Chloe said. "You have a date, don't you?"

"I—"

"You do!" Delilah squealed. "With who?"

"The general manager and it's not a date." This was why she didn't want to talk. Because Chloe and Delilah would force her to face reality. "Have the two of you forgotten that I'm here on my honeymoon?"

"Without your groom," Chloe shot back.

"Thank you for reminding me." Immediately, Larissa regretted snapping. Since Carlos appeared on her walkway two nights ago, she'd hadn't thought of Tom once, and she'd barely thought of him before that.

"All I meant was that you shouldn't feel bad if you want to have a little fun while you're south of the border."

"Who said I feel bad?" she asked. If anything, she'd felt way too good the past few days.

"So long as you don't let all those romantic sunsets go to your head."

"What's that supposed to mean?" She didn't like the way Delilah's comment made the hair on her neck stand up.

"It means don't get too carried away. You know what a sucker you are when it comes to romance."

"For goodness' sake, Delilah, I just broke my engagement. I'm not looking for a deep relationship." Even as she said the words, however, she could hear the distant warning bells. Suggesting she might remind herself of her resolve a little more frequently.

"Give the woman a break, wouldn't you, Del? She's going to dinner, not running away with the guy. Don't listen to her, La-Roo. The only advice you need is to not do anything we wouldn't do."

Talk about loose guidance. When it came to caution, the two women were at complete opposite ends of the spectrum. "Pretty wide berth, don't you think?"

"Plenty of wiggle room for a good time," her friend replied.

"Good Lord, there's going to be a chef and a launch operator with us. How much wiggling do you think there's going to be?"

"Depends on how creative a thinker you are. You'd be amazed what you can do when you think outside the box."

"Very amusing." She wondered if Chloe would give the same advice if she knew how much *wiggling* she and Carlos had done already.

After a few more minutes of conversation, mostly about the hotel and her room, and one last warning from Delilah to keep her head, Larissa hung up. Immediately, a server showed up to top off her coffee. Invisible, discreet service. Carlos would be pleased to see his dictate being carried out with such efficiency.

Mug cradled in her hands, she let it hover below her lips while she stared at the horizon. The sky and water met with perfect complimentary colors. Dark navy abutting cerulean. So much of Mexico's colors seemed plucked from a box of crayons. Bright, bold, beautiful.

Romantic as sin.

Delilah's remark about Mexican sunsets nagged. Everyone always teased her about being overly romantic. *Addicted to romance,* Chloe liked to say. *All those years helping your grandmother gave you tulle on the brain.*

Was it possible she was letting her surroundings color her emotions? Would Carlos's kisses be as intoxicating if they took place somewhere like the corner of Fifty-ninth and Madison? Did it even matter? In a few days, she'd be back on Madison Avenue, while Carlos stayed here. Was it really important for her to know the answer?

Wow, she thought, setting her coffee down. For a woman whose ex-fiancé accused her of not having deep thoughts, she was certainly thinking herself into a corner, wasn't she?

"I heard you booked the open moonlight cruise."

Carlos looked from his paperwork to see his cousin who stood in the doorway. "That's right, I did. For Señorita Boyd."

"And for you, as well."

"She mentioned the cruise had been a highly anticipated part of her old itinerary. I thought taking advantage of the cancellation would be a nice way to show our appreciation for her help."

"Interesting. I would have thought visiting her room the past two nights would be message enough."

Carlos washed his hands over his face. He'd been wondering how long before Jorge said something. His staff might be discreet, but they weren't blind. Nor had he been overly secretive about his rendezvous. Sighing, he got up and went to shut the door. "You could at least keep your voice down."

"Little late to be worried about discretion now,

don't you think? The time to worry was before you decided to mix business with pleasure."

Carlos winced.

"Regardless, I'd prefer to at least try and protect the señorita's reputation."

"Relax, *primo,* I made sure we were alone before I said anything. I don't want to encourage gossip any more than you do."

"Gracias."

"No need to thank me. I'm happy to see you finally moving on."

"I'm not moving on." The response was reflexive.

"Then what are you doing?"

"I…" Carlos wasn't sure. He certainly didn't set out to become Larissa's lover. Quite the opposite. The other afternoon, he'd decided to take a drive precisely because he wanted to clear his head of the notion. *Until he saw her sitting on the curb.* From that moment on, kissing her had been inevitable, and after kissing…well, there was no turning back. He could no more stop himself from going to her room than he could stop breathing. His actions were no longer his own.

Jorge, if he heard such an explanation, would never let it go, so Carlos settled for a half-truth instead. "We're two people enjoying each other's company, that is all."

"Well, I have to say, you've got good taste. She is a beautiful woman. She must be very special, too, to get your attention after all these years."

You don't know by half. Leaving Larissa each morning proved increasingly difficult. She was sweet, smart and had an uncanny ability for making him feel lighter. By the end with Mirabelle, he'd had a persistent weight pressing down on him. For the first time in years, he didn't feel the pressure.

"Don't read too much into the situation," he told Jorge. Or was he telling himself? "She's only here for a few more days."

"If I remember correctly, you courted, proposed and married Mirabelle in the same amount of time."

And look where that got him. "Larissa is not Mirabelle."

"Thank goodness."

Spine stiffening, Carlos turned away. On other

side of the glass the ocean looked particularly blue today. Perhaps he'd take a perimeter walk. Clear his head. *Because doing so worked so well the last time....*

Behind him, the leather guest chair crinkled as Jorge shifted his weight. His cousin gearing up for another comment. How foolish for him to think the conversation over. He held his breath, waiting for what he knew was coming.

"What happened to Mirabelle wasn't your fault. No one could have loved her more than you if they tried."

And yet he still failed her. Did his cousin ever stop to think that Carlos might not want to fail again? Some mistakes were too awful to repeat. The most he and Larissa could ever be were two people incredibly and insatiably attracted to one another.

Not that more could happen anyway. Even if he were capable of having a deeper relationship, come the end of the week, Larissa would leave for New York, and their affair would be in the past. Which, he thought rubbing a sudden pang in his sternum, was exactly what he wanted.

* * *

"Why is it women always keep us waiting?"

Carlos shot the chef a look. "I would hardly call five minutes a wait," he replied.

"*Lo siento, señor.* It seemed longer."

Yes, thought Carlos, it did. Fortunately, his employees knew better than to call him on the fact the launch arrived at Larissa's villa ten minutes early and coasted around the lagoon to kill time.

Turning so his back was to the boat, he wiped his hands on his slacks. "I'm sure the señorita will be outside any moment."

"She's outside now," Larissa said.

She hustled toward him, wearing a curve-hugging red dress and platform sandals. As he watched her hips swing back and forth, Carlos's mouth began to water.

"Sorry I made you wait," she said, her voice breathy. "I ran into Paul and Linda by the pool. We ended up talking about tomorrow's ceremony and the time slipped away."

He couldn't care less about Linda Stevas. The only thing he could think about was how much Larissa's body resembled an hourglass, and how he couldn't wait to run his hands over every blessed inch of time. *Two people incredibly and insatiably attracted to one another.*

Suddenly the launch was over capacity by two. "Disembark," he barked at the crew. "I'll handle the boat from here."

Both staff members' mouths opened. "But this is the VIP section. How are we supposed to get back to the main hotel?"

"Call for another launch." There were plenty of boats still available. "Or walk." So long as they didn't set sail with them. The men grumbled but did as he requested. Tomorrow there would be gossip, but at the moment, Carlos couldn't be bothered to care. The gleam in Larissa's eyes told him that neither could she.

He held out his hand. "Ready to board?"

It didn't surprise Larissa that Carlos could maneuver the launch on his own or that he looked completely in command standing at the wheel in his suit. Everything the man did oozed confidence; why shouldn't steering a boat?

Lifting a hand from the wheel, he slipped an

arm around her waist. "You're standing too far away," he said. The hum of the engine required that he bring his mouth close to her ear so when he spoke, his lips tickled the outer shell. Larissa shivered.

"How about I open the bottle I saw chilling?" she whispered back, slipping from his grip. Ever since the boat pulled to the dock, her insides had been a jittery mess, more in keeping with a first date than two people who'd been sharing a bed for days. After the things Carlos and she had done the past two nights, that she should feel any shyness was absurd. For goodness' sake, didn't she pour herself in to this dress knowing full well what kind of message it telegraphed? A message Carlos received loud and clear, she might add.

The nerves were Delilah's fault. Her comment about not getting carried away kept replaying itself. The warning was completely unnecessary; both Larissa and Carlos understood the parameters of their *relationship.* She wasn't about to build their affair into anything more. Didn't matter how gorgeous and romantic the setting.

Unlike the regular launches, which featured

rows of benches to accommodate multiple passengers, the dinner boats had counter space and cooking equipment. A gauzy curtain divided the stern from the rest of the space, so guests could maintain the illusion of being alone of the water. Since she and Carlos really were alone, the curtain remained open. She made her way to where the ice bucket sat on the floor next to the cushioned bench seat. The bottle had already been opened and left to breathe.

"I see, you're going to make me break my no-alcohol rule," she teased over her shoulder.

"What?"

No sense talking over the engine. Clearly, conversation would have to wait. She lifted the bottle only to stare at the label in surprise. *Spring water.* Carlos must have directed the chef to replace the usual wine for her sake.

How silly, getting a lump in her throat over a bottle of water, but there it was, thick and large, and causing her chest to grow tight.

"Everything all right?" Carlos called back.

Everything was great. Pouring two glasses, she made her way back to his side.

Carlos steered the boat west to where an inlet divided the jungle into two before cutting the ending. From there, they floated in silence toward the trees, where the last rays of sunlight broke through toward the water. "I'm afraid this is the best sunset I can do given how they built the resort," he told her. "You would get a far better view from the oceanside."

"It's perfect," Larissa told him. Handing off one of the glasses, she used her free hand to pull him close for a deep kiss. "Thank you," she whispered against his lips.

"If this is how you thank me for an obstructed sunset, perhaps I should arrange for a glass-bottomed boat cruise so you can see the real deal." He swiped his thumb over her lower lip, a tease in comparison to the mouth hovering near hers. "Of course, on an ocean cruise, we wouldn't have as much privacy. My boating skills are limited to small launches."

"I can't believe you told your employees to leave."

"Would you rather I'd asked them to stay?"

"They're going to talk."

"They are already."

"And you don't mind?" He never did address her comment from earlier.

"Naturally, I'd prefer they didn't. For your sake, as much as mine."

"You're trying to protect my reputation."

"Shouldn't I?" he asked, thumbing her lip again.

"Is that why you leave before dawn?"

A look flashed in his eyes, but he shuttered them before she could decipher what it meant. "Ah, *querida,* I'm not keeping you a secret if that's what you're asking."

"Then…"

"Because if I waited until you woke up, we'd stay in bed all day."

That wasn't the reason; the fearful flash she saw said as much, but before she could challenge him, Carlos bent his head and nipped, vampire-like, at the curve of her neck. "Have I mentioned how incredibly beautiful you look in that dress?" It was a distraction of the finest order, because Larissa's knees immediately buckled. She'd let him skate by for now, but promised herself that at some point, she'd find out the truth.

"There is one problem," he whispered, after a moment.

"A problem?" She found it hard to think clearly when his lips were exploring. "What's that?"

"I may have dismissed the chef prematurely."

"In other words, we don't have anything to eat on our dinner cruise." Larissa started to giggle. She couldn't help herself. The unplanned nature of his confession, implying he'd been too over-whelmed by her to think clearly, only made the evening more romantic. Pulling back the curtain, she saw for the first time, the containers of food neatly stacked on the counters. "It shouldn't be too difficult to whip something up."

"You know how to cook Yucatán cuisine?"

"No, but I can turn on a stove."

Laughing at Carlos' expression, she began peeking in containers. "We've got marinating meat, chopped vegetables, beans, spices. Might not be authentic, but we can throw something to-gether. Sort of a Yucatán stir-fry?"

"Carnita," he said, over her shoulder.

"That's a much better word. How is it every-thing sounds so much more exotic in Spanish?"

"You only think that because it's a foreign lan-guage."

"A foreign language where people roll their *R*s. *Car-r-r-rnita*." She imitated his pronunciation. "I love how the words drip off the tongue."

"Just words, *querida?*"

Heat flooded her from head to toe. He'd added the Spanish endearment on purpose for that exact reason, she bet. "Cook," she said, directing him to the stove.

While the meal wasn't authentic or even close to gourmet, they managed to mix the ingredi-ents into an edible concoction. Carlos also found a fruit platter and prepared appetizers in the re-frigerator. More than enough to make a satisfy-ing meal.

They ate from a shared plate, forgoing the dining table in favor of sitting side by side on the bench, forks and hips invading each other's space. While cooking slowed the physical part of the night, it lent an added layer of intimacy. There was a teamwork required of cooking that made Larissa feel as connected to him as she had during their nights together.

With the sun gone, the jungle had turned black, leaving only the light from the boat reflecting off the watter. Her interest in food long gone, Larissa leaned against Carlos' shoulder and listened to the waves as they lapped against the launch. Somewhere in the darkness, an animal screeched.

"Monkey," Carlos said, teasing her lips with a piece of papaya. "They live in the canopy. If you watch long enough, you'll catch one swinging across the branches."

"Sure don't see that in New York. In fact, you don't see any of this in New York. Just buildings. Lots and lots of buildings." Her sigh sounded overly loud thanks to the silence. "You don't get this kind of quiet in the city, either."

"Sounds like Mexico has cast a spell on someone."

"Maybe Mexico has." *Or someone in Mexico.* Delilah's warning whispered in her ear.

"Well, there's always the wedding coordinator position here at the resort if you want to stay."

"Tonight, your offer is very tempting." Only it wouldn't be the job luring her to stay.

"I know something else that is very tempting." Carlos's breath tickled her cheek as he leaned close to press kisses along her jaw. Fingers cupped her chin, turning her face to his. His tongue flickered over her lips, tasting, teasing. "Why is it I can't get enough of you?" he asked her.

Larissa had been asking herself the same question. Everything about Carlos—the way he moved, the way he spoke, his very existence—was like an aphrodisiac. He'd spoiled her for other men. And now, to top it off, looking into his eyes she saw a tenderness that took her breath away.

She combed her fingers through his thick curls. Maybe she was falling for a fantasy, but right now, she didn't care. Reality was overrated. "Do you need an answer?" she asked him?

"No," he replied. "Not tonight." He lowered his mouth to hers.

"Tell me about her."

Nestled against his chest, Larissa felt him

stiffen. He didn't like the question, but she needed to ask. From the moment the two of them began this attraction, there'd been a third presence in the room. Mirabelle's ghost clung to Carlos. She was the distance Larissa felt when they made love, and the reason for his shuttered expression. After giving herself so freely, Larissa felt she deserved to know more about the woman who kept her from getting closer.

"I don't know what tell you," he replied.

"You said she was beautiful. Start there."

His laugh was soft, sad. "Women. Always comparing. Yes, she was very beautiful. First time I saw her, I swore my heart stopped beating. I decided then and there I wanted to spend the rest of my life with her. We married three days later."

Three days. The same length of time they'd been together. The coincidence stung. "Love at first sight."

"*Si.*" What was it he said in the *cenote?* Mirabelle had been the center of his universe? Larissa shoved the tightness in her chest aside. If she didn't want the answer, she shouldn't have asked the question.

"How long were you married before she got sick?"

Again, he stiffened. "I think she was sick all along. I didn't see the signs, is all. We seemed so happy in the beginning. Everything was such a whirlwind. The rush of falling in love had us high for weeks. But eventually, it wore off. I tried to keep her happy, but…" His voice drifted off, despair hanging heavy in the words he didn't say, and it was then Larissa realized Mirabelle's sickness hadn't been physical. She wrapped her arms tighter about his waist. If she held him close enough, perhaps she could soften the hurt. "What happened?" she asked. The hair on the back of her neck stood on edge. Maybe she didn't want to know.

"She drowned," Carlos replied. "In the pool."

Dear Lord. She expected something about fighting or their struggle with mental illness, not such a blunt, flat answer. "I'm so sorry," she whispered.

"Jorge and I found her. We tried to revive her, but it was too late." His body trembled along with his voice. "She'd been drinking heavily those last few days. The authorities said she probably tripped and her legs became tangled in the gown she was wearing."

In her list of imagined horrors, drowning was one of the worst. Your body screaming for air. Nothing but water filling your lungs. How the poor woman must have suffered. No wonder he'd been so frightened when housekeeping called him to her room.

There was more to the story; she could tell because Carlos's body had grown tenser than ever. With her heart in her throat, Larissa held on tight and waited for him to go on.

When he did, his voice was barely above a whisper. "She was a strong swimmer."

Larissa sat up. "I don't…" Understand? But she did; she simply didn't want to contemplate. "Are you saying she deliberately…?" She couldn't even say the words.

Carlos shook his head. "She was so unhappy. I tried—we all tried so hard—but nothing every worked. The darkness, the insecurities, they always won."

"Oh, Carlos." Larissa couldn't imagine living

with such uncertainty. Carrying all that grief and guilt. No wonder he emanated such pain. She'd only heard his story, and her own heart ached on his behalf.

"You can't know for certain," she said. Cradling his jaw, she forced him to meet her eyes so he could see the reassurance she so badly wanted him to feel. "It still could have been an accident. The authorities—they have ways of knowing what happened. They'd know if…"

"If she got tired of trying?" He brushed the hair from her face, his hand coming to rest in a mirror image of her own. "You're right, *querida.* We will never know for sure. It doesn't matter. I hate her all the same."

"What?" The harshness caught her off guard. How could he hate the woman who owned his heart?

Giving her forehead a kiss, Carlos eased himself away from her. The absence of his body made the bench a cold and lonely place, and she drew her knees close to stay warm. She watched as he poured himself a glass of water, graceful

even in distress. "I suppose you think I'm heart-
less for saying so."

"I— No."

"You don't?"

"No, I don't."

In fact, she understood better than he realized
the questions those left behind were stuck dealing
with. Why did she leave? Weren't you enough to
make her happy? Hadn't she asked all those questions herself as a child? When a person walked
away, the betrayal lingered.

"You're angry with her."

"*Angry* is not a strong enough word for what I
feel." He jammed the bottle into the melted ice.
"I loved her. I *worshiped* her. But my love wasn't
enough. She always needed more. Excitement,
fireworks. She wanted the honeymoon to never
end, and I obliged. I gave and I gave until I was
drained dry. And it still wasn't enough. I wasn't
enough." The sentence came out close to a sob.

Her poor, poor Carlos. His cynicism made
sense now. How else could he feel when he gave
his heart, only to come up short.

"I was such a fool," he said. "I believed love

would solve everything. But no. Love does nothing. And now…" He looked away with a sigh. "And now, I can't love anyone anymore. I'm empty."

"No," Larissa whispered. "That's not true."

"Yes, *querida*. I am. Best I can do is a night like this."

A wonderful, magical night. He wasn't empty. Far from it. The ache in her heart shifted, deepened. If only she could make him see. Knew the right words to say. She opened her mouth, but inspiration didn't come.

Without words, she'd have to use the next best thing. She closed the space between them. He looked so beautiful standing in the dim light, his skin streaked by shadows. Unable not to, she traced the patterns with her finger. Across his collarbone, down his breastbone. The beat of his heart rose up through his skin to greet her. Strong, full. Not empty at all.

For three days, she'd been standing on the edge of an emotional crevasse, and now the gap wrenched open, propelling her over the edge. She pressed her lips against the sound, and gifted his heart with her own.

A groan broke the silence. Carlos's hands tangled in her hair. "Larissa…"

She held him tight, and prayed for Mirabelle to disappear.

Morning was streaming through the mango branches when Carlos pulled the launch to Larissa's villa. Long—long—past when the other cruises had returned.

Standing in the cabin doorway, Larissa hugged her coffee mug, and watched as he neatly abutted the dock. "You were right," she told him. "Café D'orzo is way better than regular coffee. I'm going to have to tell Chloe's boyfriend to add it to the coffee shop menu. He can call it Carlos's Special."

The specter of a smile graced Carlos's mouth. Since they woke up, awkwardness had hung between them, heavy and uncomfortable, more in keeping with a one-night stand than two people who shared an intimate encounter. Their lovemaking had been open and honest, but immediately afterwards, Carlos closed down. Regretting he'd shared too much or afraid of the way he let Larissa in? Most likely both.

There was a soft bump as boat met wood. "Guess this means the moonlight cruise has come to an end," she said.

"Seeing as how the moonlight ended a few hours ago, I'd say so." He took the coffee cup from her hands, then pulled her in for a cinnamon-flavored kiss. The ardor was the same as always, along with his guarded expression. She'd so hoped things might have changed.

Since they only had a couple days left, she decided it was better to go with what they had than push a fight. "Sleep well?"

"When you finally let me sleep."

"Let you sleep? I wasn't the one demanding thirds." She smacked his shoulder. This, they could do. Banter and light conversation.

"I was simply going the extra mile to keep my guest happy."

His teasing stung more than it should, largely because, after his confession, Larissa wasn't sure he didn't partially mean what he was saying. The line delineating commitment and casual still existed, and she remained planted firmly on the temporary side.

A voice in her head reminded her she should be fine with the position. *You're not looking for more, remember?*

She turned to topics more practical to keep from listening. "Thank you for the jacket. It made for a very comfortable blanket."

"You mean I wasn't enough?"

Pink crept into her cheeks. "Would you like to come in?" she asked. "You know, to shower before work?"

"Oh, *querida,* if only I could." He brushed her cheek with the back of his hand, igniting the now familiar shivers. "But I need to return the boat to the boathouse before people on the staff start to wonder what happened."

Of course, he did. Thank goodness for convenient excuses. Larissa kept her disappointment to herself. At least now she understood his reasons. Maybe after she got some sleep, she wouldn't take the rejection so personally.

"It's just as well," she replied. "I wanted to head

over to the resort to check on preparations for Paul's and Linda's ceremony later this morning anyway."

"You don't have to do that. I'm sure catering will have everything well in hand."

"I want to." She was invested in the couple having the perfect ceremony. "Will I see you there? At the ceremony?"

"I'll be by."

"Good. Maybe we could steal a dance." As much as it killed her, she managed a smile as she rose on tiptoes and kissed his cheek. "Thank you for last night. I couldn't ask for a better memory."

"Larissa, I—" She gasped as he gripped her shoulders. His dark eyes searched her face. He was on the edge, she could feel him struggling to open up. Instead, he kissed her long and hard. When she tasted his desperation, Larissa knew he'd backed away. "I'll see you at the ceremony," he told her.

She waited in her doorway as he steered the launch back toward the center of the lagoon. After tomorrow, she'd never see Carlos again.

She'd leave him and paradise behind. Her heart began to splinter.

Delilah's warning sounded. *Don't let the atmosphere go to your head.* Larissa had a very bad feeling she'd failed to listen.

It wasn't technically a lie. Carlos did have to return the launch to the boathouse. It simply wasn't the real reason he rushed off. Staring at the sky half the night didn't clear his head. If anything, he seemed to be losing his grip.

Once Larissa was safely in her villa, he pulled away from the dock. He intended to drive straight to the boathouse, but when he reached the center of the lagoon, he suddenly cut the engine, letting the early morning silence envelop him. Perhaps the quiet would settle his thoughts.

Last night was… He didn't know what to call it. A rawness assaulted his body as if he'd been cut open and his insides exposed to the world. Certainly, he didn't expect their lovemaking to feel so intimate. Or for him to share so much of himself. The latter he blamed on the former. Larissa's arms gave him courage and before he could stop, his history with Mirabelle poured out. The exchange left him torn in two, with one half wanting nothing more than to lose himself in Larissa forever while the other screamed to push her away.

Closing his eyes, he saw Larissa's blue gaze. So full of comfort and reassurance. An indefinable longing gripped his soul. The desperate sensation reminded him of the days when he first met Mirabelle. Those heady, infatuated days of new love he swore would never happen again.

Fear squeezed at his chest. They *wouldn't* happen again. They *couldn't*. He'd only fail, and Larissa was far too special for him to hurt.

CHAPTER NINE

"WAIT! ISN'T IT supposed to be the red flowers at the top of the altar and purple on the bottom?" The shaman had been very specific about the flowers position. Last thing she wanted to do was give Paul and Linda bad energy because they stuck the tulipanes in the wrong location.

Larissa took out her phone and double-checked the compass app she downloaded earlier. She was right. North was indeed the top of the altar. *Phew.* She smiled at the workers, who she was pretty sure didn't understand a word she said, and switched the flower positions herself. Catering was setting up early to allow the shaman to purify the altar in advance of the ceremony. That way, Paul and Linda wouldn't have any lingering smoke.

She arranged the flowers around the candle, stepped back, then arranged the flowers again.

You'd think she was the one getting married, she was being so obsessive with details. Delilah and Chloe would be making Bridezilla comments left and right.

Thing was, she liked wedding details. She liked planning weddings. A lifetime of listening to brides-to-be left their mark because she took pleasure in the nitty-gritty details. Stressing about seating numbers was way more fun than typing media contracts and coordinating sales department meetings. The only fun she had with those was trying to top the previous meeting's snack menu.

Besides, obsessing over these details kept her from fixating on Carlos.

I hate her. All morning, she replayed the painful declaration. She was pretty sure he didn't truly hate his late wife, even if there was a thin line dividing the emotion from love. The anguish lacing his voice had been too strong. She couldn't begin to imagine what life must have been like for him during those years. Loving a woman so deeply only to see her slip away to depression.

Her eyes began to water. They'd been doing

that a lot this morning. Blinking rapidly, she turned away from the workers so they wouldn't notice. If they did, she'd blame the sand. On the other side of the beach, near the pool, she spied a familiar figure talking to one of the assistant managers. If they were in a movie, he'd sense her presence, and their eyes would meet. Being real life, however, Larissa found herself watching while he spoke. Did Carlos have any idea how captivating a figure he made? How much strength he exuded merely by standing still? Larissa smiled. She bet Mirabelle fell in love with him at first sight, as well.

Carlos said something and the other manager smiled. Beamed actually, like he'd paid her the biggest compliment in the world. Who wouldn't? Carlos's attention would make anyone feel special. Damn Mirabelle's demons for letting Carlos think his devotion wasn't enough.

"Did the flower do something to upset you?" Paul Stevas suddenly appeared at her shoulder.

Looking down, Larissa saw she was crushing a tulipane in her fist. "Keeping a firm hand, is all. If you don't show flowers who's boss, they'll run amok," she told him. Hopefully her cheeks weren't too flushed.

Speaking of flushed, Paul was red and sweaty himself. Back from running the beach, no doubt. "Let me guess, Linda threw you out."

"She, her mom and my mom were doing some sort of spa thing up in the room," he replied. "Minute I saw the nail polish, I was out of there."

"Wise choice. While I'm pretty sure the bad luck before the wedding rule only applies to couples who aren't already married, you're still smart to stay clear of her until she's ready."

"Believe me, I know. I didn't survive a year of marriage without learning something."

Larissa laughed. "By the way, Linda showed me a picture of her dress. She's going to look gorgeous."

"Hope so. I know she won't be happy unless she looks perfect in the pictures. I wish I could get her to realize I don't care what she wears. To me, she'll always look beautiful." Using the hem of his shirt as a towel, he wiped the sheen in his voice, although with the way his voice cracked at the end of his sentence, he might have well been wiping his eyes. If the day's emotions were getting to him this early, heaven help him when they reached the actual ceremony.

"If Linda's having a spa day, I guess that means she didn't get sick after all. I heard you two took a trip to the emergency room," she added when Paul looked at her.

"Did she tell you why?"

"Only that she had a little trouble breathing."

"I was afraid she was having a pleural effusion."

"A what?"

"Sorry, I forget not everyone lives with medical speak. It's a kind of breathing complication people can get when they have lung cancer."

"Linda has cancer?" Larissa's stomach dropped. No wonder the poor girl looked so frail.

"Stage four," Paul said in a soft voice. "Untreatable. We decided to stop treatment and go for quality of life for however long she has left."

But she was so young. Larissa felt sick. "I'm sorry." Unable to say anything else, she stared at the crumpled flower.

"Thanks," Paul replied. "It's been a long couple years. We actually thought we might lose her last year, so she and I got married while she was in the hospital. Linda says she didn't care, but I know she did. She'd always wanted a big fancy wedding, ever since we first talked about getting married."

Which was why he wanted to pull out all the stops this year. This trip was their last hurrah. Here Carlos thought Paul was a lovesick fool spending himself into debt, when in actuality, he and Linda were creating one last, amazing memory. Larissa's eyes began to water again.

Immediately, Paul was in front of her, fussing and patting imaginary pockets for a tissue. "I'm sorry. I didn't mean to upset you. Sometimes the story pops out before I've had a chance to think."

"Please, don't apologize," Larissa told him. *Don't ever apologize for being that much in love.* "I think it's wonderful that the two of you are making up for the missed opportunity."

"Are you kidding? Linda's my world. I'd do anything for her."

"I'm sure you would," Larissa murmured. Paul reminded her of someone else she knew. A man who'd been willing to give his wife the moon if it made her happy. How ironic that the man whose wife had a whole life in front of her didn't appreciate the effort while the woman who didn't…

For the first time in days, Tom popped into her head and all of a sudden, Larissa felt very unworthy.

"My father and father-in-law are waiting on me in the restaurant. I should go meet them," she heard Paul say. "Is there anything I need to do here?"

She shook her head. "Señor Chavez and his staff have everything under control."

"It's important everything to be perfect."

"It will be. Let the resort worry about the details. The only thing you need to worry about is enjoying yourself."

Funny that she would tell Paul not to stress about details. She who changed wedding venues three times and gave new meaning to the term *wedding obsessed.* Her sense of unworthiness swelled larger. All that time and effort planning the perfect ceremony. Would she have chucked all her plans if Tom—or she—had gotten sick?

For that matter, would she have moved heaven and earth to make her partner happy the way Paul did? The way Carlos did?

The answers came back a resounding no on all counts. Tom, it appeared, had been right again. The man was still a jerk for cheating on her, but he also had a point. How many times had he tried to get her to dial back her plans, to talk about something other than the wedding. But as far as she was concerned, it had been all wedding, all the time. She was so happy someone wanted to marry her—that she was going to finally get to be a bride—she didn't stop to think about what was really important.

She really did love the wedding details more than she'd loved him.

Paul and Linda, Delilah and her husband, Simon, even Chloe and her boyfriend Ian—they had real love. You need only look at their faces to see how much they cared for one another. Oh, sure, she'd loved Tom, but never with the bone-deep intensity the others did.

Or the way she felt when she was with Carlos.

Flower petals dropped to the floor. She could

not be in love with Carlos. Being drawn to the man did not make her in love, no matter how deeply his story touched her, or how badly she wanted his heart to heal.

No, that was attraction, concern, infatuation. Like Delilah said, it was the atmosphere playing tricks with her emotions. For crying out loud, she'd known the man for a few days. The only people she'd ever heard of falling in love that quickly were Simon and Delilah. And Chloe and Ian.

Carlos and his first wife.

Oh, damn, was she in trouble. She needed to have a good long think and figure out where her mind was truly at.

First, though, she needed to make an international phone call. She owed Tom a very big apology. Then, she would figure out the rest of her feelings.

The ceremony went off flawlessly. Husband and wife were beaming as they held hands before the floral altar. Their parents offered sacrifices of fruits and vegetables and lit candles to represent each point of the compass. Then the shaman had them proclaim their commitment to one another "…for as long as the commitment lasts."

As she listened to Linda repeat the shaman's translated vows, Larissa felt a tear slip down her cheek. Weddings always made her cry. At Simon and Delilah's she'd bawled like a baby. This ceremony of two virtual strangers hit her far harder.

Paul and Linda were so brave. The depth of their courage and love amazed her. They didn't need all the bells and whistles to prove they belonged to one another. They simply did.

That, thought Larissa, was what she wanted next time around. Not a big fancy wedding, but a marriage. For richer or poorer, in sickness and in health. She sniffed back another tear.

There was only one problem: She wasn't sure a second time around would ever happen. A real relationship required two fully committed hearts, and she had the sinking feeling her heart had gone and found a mate that refused to open his.

She stole a look to her right. Carlos's face was as handsome and unreadable as ever as he watched Paul and Linda seal their vows with a kiss. Just once before she left for home, Larissa wished he would look at her with clear, unguarded eyes. A pipe dream, she knew. She'd come close last night, and yet even then, when sharing his darkest secret, Carlos still refused to fully let her in. If he couldn't open his heart at his most vulnerable, what made her think he ever could?

Leave it to her to come on her honeymoon nursing a bruised ego and return home with a worse broken heart than before.

Their vows complete, Paul and Linda turned to the altar where the shaman lit the center candle, the merging of male and female. Maybe it was because she knew Paul and Linda's story, but the moment held a profound solemnity. Looking around, she saw that she wasn't the only one affected. Both sets of parents were openly weeping, as well. The true meaning of what they were all witnessing hung heavy in the air.

When the ceremony ended, she was the one hugging Linda for a change. "I don't know why you were worried about looking bad in the photographs. You look so beautiful," she told her. It was true. The peasant dress camouflaged her skinniness while someone, her mother, maybe, had taken extra care with her makeup so that she looked radiant and healthy. Her visible happiness helped with the glow, too. "Are you happy with how the ceremony turned out?"

"Are you kidding? Everything turned out better than I could have ever imagined."

"I'm glad," Larissa told her. "You deserve a memorable afternoon." She was trying not to get weepy, but it was difficult.

Apparently she failed, for the young woman met her eyes with a long look that said, "You know, don't you?" The only answer Larissa could give was to squeeze her hands.

Paul slipped up behind his wife to kiss her on the cheek. "Hey, babe, your mom wants to take some group shots in front of the altar."

"Again? Good Lord, how many shots of the same scenery does she need?" Linda asked. She was smiling, however, as she rolled her eyes. "Will you excuse us?"

"Congratulations, *querida*. Your ceremony was a success."

She watched Carlos approach, wondering if

there'd ever come a time when she didn't marvel at the way he moved. "Not my ceremony," she told him. "Your catering staff did all the work."

"Yes, but you provided the inspiration." He handed her a goblet of golden liquid. Xtabentún. In an oddly prescient moment, she suggested the Mayan liquor yesterday to toast to Paul and Linda's health and happiness. Lord knew the two of them could use all the good vibes they could get.

"Plus," he continued, "you were down here first thing supervising the arrangements when you could have been home catching up on your sleep."

"I wasn't that tired."

"No? Then I must be losing my touch." His smile was full of wicked promise as he tapped the rim of his glass to hers. "Regardless, I am very impressed. This is exactly the kind of ceremony that made La Joya's reputation. It's traditional, it's memorable—"

"Magical?"

"Exactly," he replied. "You've definitely raised the bar when it comes to hiring a new wedding coordinator."

"Too bad I'm only temporary, right?"

The sour tone slipped out before she could stop herself. Too bad. She didn't feel much in the mood for compliments right now. Especially when they both knew how meaningless his comments were.

She raised her glass only to wrinkle her nose at the sweet scent. Between the flowers and the fruit, the air was cloying enough. A tight ball found its way behind her left eye where it throbbed every time she inhaled. She needed fresh air.

Actually, she thought, as Carlos's warm presence abutted her, she needed space. Having him close only made her head worse.

The shoreline stood only a few feet away, but it was downwind enough to feel like miles. Setting her drink on a nearby table, she made her way past the tide line to the water's edge. Damp sand slid between her toes reminding her of the other night, and Carlos's lesson about the tides. How different this trip might have been if she hadn't agreed to help him that night. If, instead of insisting on enjoying her wedding dinner, she'd hid in her room.

She heard Carlos making his way through the sand. No surprise there. Her departure had been abrupt. "Is something wrong, *querida?*"

"A little headache, is all."

"See? You are tired. Would you like me to take you back to your room?"

So he could make her feel like the only woman in the world for another few hours? Tempting, but after witnessing Paul and Linda's courage, she wasn't in the mood for indulging in fantasy. "I'll be fine in a few minutes," she told him.

His hands settled on her shoulders, his fingers gently kneading. "If you change your mind," he whispered as his thumbs pressed the muscles on either side of her spine, "I know a way to help you relax."

Temptation won for a moment, and her eyes fluttered shut. She would miss this, his touch. Unless…

"What would you do if I told you I wanted to stay?" she asked.

"You just did, *querida.*"

"No, I mean stay at La Joya. Take you up on your offer to be the wedding coordinator."

The hands stopped moving. "I—"

That's what she thought. "Don't worry," she said, pulling away, "I wasn't serious. We both know my staying would completely mess up your plans."

"Plans?"

"Sure. I mean, you can't keep having a fling with your wedding coordinator, can you? Your predecessor already took care of that. Far better I leave and never come back. This way you don't have to worry about any messy loose ends, right?"

Carlos looked utterly confused. "What are you talking about? I never had any plans. You were always leaving at the end of the week."

"Exactly." Her head started to pound. Maybe she was overtired after all. She was being childish and surly when he'd done nothing but be honest from the start. Wasn't his fault she fell for him. "Forget I said anything. I'm being overly emotional. Paul and Linda…"

"Did something happen?"

Something, all right. She looked him in the eye. "She's dying."

"Who?"

"Linda. She has lung cancer. Paul told me this morning. That's why he went to all this trouble. For one last memory."

The color drained from his face. He muttered something in Spanish. Soft, but from the sharpness, Larissa knew it was some kind of obscenity.

She turned her attention to the horizon. "Doesn't seem fair, does it? Both so young and in love."

"Poor bastard would be better off if he never fell in love in the first place."

Larissa's insides died a little. He really believed that, didn't he? It broke her heart.

Spying a half-buried seashell, she dug it free with her big toe. Immediately the tide sent the shell tumbling end over end. She scooped it up, letting the sharp edges dig into her palm.

"Growing up, I used to watch the women getting their fittings," she said. "No matter who they were or what they looked like, the minute they put on the dress, they transformed. They were beautiful. Everyone would gather around and fuss over them."

In a flash she was back in her grandmother's living room. A poor, chubby, motherless girl surrounded by white satin and sequins. "It was like they'd become princesses. I always figured that someday I'd put on a white dress and become a princess, too. Then I'd live happily ever after. Like in the movies.

"Except it's not about the dress, is it?" she asked, turning to him. "It's about what the dress represents. What the whole wedding represents. Loving the person with all your heart."

"Love isn't the answer, either."

"I hate that you think that way." Then again, that was the whole crux of their problem, wasn't it? She'd chuck all the romance in the world to have him think differently.

"Why shouldn't I?" he asked her. "I loved Mirabelle. I loved her with all my heart and what did it mean? Nothing. Same with Paul and Linda. So he moved heaven and earth to give her this recommitment ceremony. She's still going to leave him.

This whole celebration means nothing. Their love means nothing."

As he spoke, the words flew faster and faster, like angry spittle hurling into the air, his tone growing so sharp it frightened her. He kicked at the sand, sending the grains flying, and that seemed to take some of the anger out of him.

"Like I said I told you, it's better to not love at all."

Maybe he was right. God knew anything would be better than the way Larissa's heart felt right now.

She looked up, hoping he could read the emotion in her eyes and understand what she was trying to tell him.

"Unfortunately, you're too late."

No... Carlos froze. She couldn't love him. He clamped down the thrill rising in his chest. "But in the *cenote,* you told me... You said that you weren't looking for a relationship."

"Apparently my heart had other ideas."

Maldita. What did he do now? Back at the top of the beach, a mariachi band had started playing. The partygoers would be dancing. Dancing to chase away the darkness. How many times had he done the same during his marriage? Too many and to what end? Larissa might see Paul's gestures as noble and romantic, but they weren't. They were foolish and painful. They could dance all they wanted, but Linda was still going to die. Paul will have failed. Like he failed Mirabelle.

Like he would eventually fail Larissa.

Icy fingers clawed at his insides, warning him to back away. He scrambled for purchase. "I told you from the start, Larissa. I don't have anything left to give. I can't love you. I can't."

Her eyes, her gorgeous, soulful eyes searched his face. "You say that, but the man I've been with the past few days... There's life inside you, Carlos. I've seen it. In the *cenote,* on the cruise."

Did she have to look so hopeful? Carlos couldn't stand to see the light in her eyes. "Those were field trips." He'd been using the same excuse all week, only the words sounded hollow this time around. "I wanted to make sure you enjoyed your visit."

"And sleeping with me? Was that another guest service?"

"No." That was him being selfish. "We agreed—"

"Stop telling me what we agreed!" Something sharp smacked his cheek. She'd thrown a seashell at his head. The ragged edge nicked the skin; he could feel the saltwater sting. "I don't want what we agreed. Not anymore."

"I can't give you anything more!" he shouted at her. Didn't she realize, what she wanted would only end up in heartache? "I was honest with you from the very start. I told you the truth."

"Did you?" she asked, calling him on his excuse. It scared him how she was starting to see through his facade. He hated the anger in her eyes, and the sadness. Seeing her in pain ripped a hole in his chest. If only they could go back to last night. When her eyes shimmered with happiness. Perhaps, if he tried, he could make her forget.

He reached for her. *"Querida..."*

"Don't!" She pushed him away before he could touch her. "I'd rather deal with reality."

She stomped away, leaving him standing alone.

CHAPTER TEN

"ACCORDING TO OUR RECORDS, Señorita Boyd, you're not scheduled to check out until tomorrow. Was there a problem?"

Larissa rested her sunglasses on top of her head. "No problem," she replied. "Just decided it was time to go home."

The clerk's expression said her excuse wasn't fooling anyone. By this point, the entire hotel had to know about her and Carlos. If not the affair, then yesterday's argument. They hadn't exactly been discreet.

Oh, well, she thought, handing over her credit card. She attracted looks checking in. She could deal with a few heading out.

The clerk typed a few keystrokes, then frowned.

"Is there a problem?" she asked.

"Uno momento, señorita. Por favor."

It was Larissa's turn to frown while he disappeared behind the rear door. Hearing him switch to Spanish made her uncomfortable. "Guess they don't like when you try to leave early," she said to the couple checking in beside her.

Clearly newlyweds, they were too wrapped up in each other to hear. Watching them whisper and exchange secret caresses made her stomach hurt. Twenty-four hours ago that had been her and Carlos. Maybe she was being stupid, taking off like this. Theirs was never supposed to be more than a few-day fling to begin with. Why let stubbornness stand in the way of their last twenty-four hours?

Because a few-days fling wasn't good enough anymore, that's why.

The rear door opened. Spying the cuff of a black suit jacket, Larissa's heart stopped. She thought for sure she wouldn't see Carlos again. After their argument on the beach, she took refuge in her room and while she hoped and hoped he'd knock on her door, he didn't.

Another reason not to extend her stay. Even if her heart could stand being around him one last day, Carlos clearly agreed the fling had ended.

What hurt the most, though, wasn't the fact that she'd developed feelings for the man, or the fact he'd walked away. It was the certainty in her heart that if Carlos had let her in, if he'd allowed himself to be close to her, that they could have had something truly spectacular. The kind of relationship she'd been searching for.

The door opened wider. The cuff became an arm, followed by a torso. Jorge.

Her heart sank. Did she really think Carlos would want to deal with her?

The assistant manager said a few quick words in Spanish to the clerk and stepped to the desk. "You're leaving us a day early, Señorita Boyd."

"Afraid so, Jorge. Manhattan calls."

Sober eyes met hers. "I'm sorry."

"Me, too," she replied. "But sometimes these things can't be helped."

After a couple silent beats, she nodded toward the computer. "Is there a problem?"

"Since we weren't expecting you to check out until tomorrow, we haven't had a chance to go over your bill. With the credits and changes Carlos made during the week, we want to make sure the charges are accurate. It will only take a moment or two." He rattled off a series of keystrokes, moved to hit Enter, and paused. "Are you sure we can't convince you to stay through tomorrow?"

Larissa shook her head. "I think I've stayed long enough. Don't worry, I promise when I give you all an online review, I won't mention our eight-legged friend. I know how Carlos likes his five-star reviews."

"He likes to know people were happy."

That he did. "Maybe too much."

"Look, I don't know what happened on the beach yesterday, but whatever happened, I'm sure Carlos didn't mean—"

"Actually," Larissa interrupted. "I'm pretty sure he did." Last night's silence confirmed the message.

"You know, he was a different person this week. More like his old self than I've seen in a long time. Not since…"

"Mirabelle? It's okay," she told the man. "Carlos told me about her."

"He did?"

Flashing back to the night on the launch, she

felt her cheeks grow warm. "I might have pushed a little."

"Ah, that makes sense." He dropped his voice. "I was with him when he found her. He was inconsolable."

Apparently she was going to get an explanation anyway. "He must have loved her very much." The words stung to say.

"*Si,* maybe too much," Jorge replied. "It scarred him when she left."

And so he drew the curtains around his heart to keep from loving too much again. That's what Larissa was afraid of.

"Hopefully someday his scars will heal," she said.

"I had hoped that's what I was seeing this week."

It was exactly what her stubborn heart didn't need to hear. Hope was hard enough to shake. Thank goodness she had sunglasses with her to hide their moisture. "Is the bill settled?" she asked, slipping them in place.

"*Si.* I'm printing you a copy now."

"Great. Could I ask one more favor? Could you

make sure Paul and Linda Stevas get this when they check out?"

Reaching into her bag, she pulled out the note she wrote last night apologizing for leaving their ceremony so abruptly and wishing them as many happy days as possible.

"I'll make a note on their file," Jorge said.

"Thank you."

Time to leave. A few more hours, and paradise would be a distant memory. Kind of already was, she thought as she started toward the door.

"You're going to leave without saying good-bye."

This time she didn't need to see a dark suit. Carlos's voice washed over her like a deep dark wave. He stood midway between the reception desk and the lobby, breathing heavy, as though he'd rushed. Was he the reason for the delay? Out of the corner of her eye, she saw Jorge disappearing back into his office.

"I'm pretty sure we said everything we had to say yesterday afternoon," she replied. Or in his case, didn't say. "I didn't think you'd care if I cut my trip short."

"Of course I—" He stopped short. Saying the word might imply feelings. "I'm sorry if my behavior led you to believe there was more to our relationship than there was. It wasn't my intention to hurt you."

"I know," Larissa replied. "But you did." See? She could be honest, too. "Don't worry, though. I bounce back. I'm nothing if not resilient."

"Querida..."

"Don't." Larissa stiffened. As far as she was concerned, he lost his right to use any endearment yesterday. *"Querida* is for a man who's brave enough to admit his feelings."

"This isn't about whether I'm brave enough."

"Oh, I know what you say it's about. You made your point very clear."

Over at the concierge desk, a pair of heads turned to look at them. She lowered her voice. "I do have to wonder, though. When exactly was it you decided your heart was too dead to have feelings for me. Was it when you spontaneously kissed me in the *cenote* or after you took me sailing in the moonlight? I'm curious because both of those are pretty sentimental activities for a guy who's dead inside.

"Goodbye, Carlos." That's what he wanted, right? A proper goodbye? Now he had one.

She got about three feet when one final thought occurred. "For the record, I didn't fall in love with you because of the moonlight. I fell for the lonely man I saw living inside you."

"Doesn't matter," Carlos whispered as he watched her march out the door. The end result was the same. "You still left."

"There's still time to get her, *primo*." Jorge appeared at his shoulder. "I could stop the taxi."

To what end? A twenty-four-hour postponement? She'd still leave. "It wouldn't make a difference."

"But you could—"

Carlos held up his hand. "Señorita Boyd is gone. Better to focus on the guests we still have."

"Next time I decide to go on a luxury vacation by myself, shoot me. Better yet, shoot me anyway." She was already miserable.

"Here." Delilah nudged Larissa's upper arm with a bowl. "This will make you feel better."

"What is it?"

"Brownie sundae. Don't tell Simon, though. It's the last brownie."

"I'll buy Simon a new batch." Larissa offered the brunette a watery smile. God bless good friends. Unable to bear going home to an empty studio, she'd been curled up on Delilah's sofa since her plane landed. "I'm sorry to intrude on you two. I figured since I crashed at Chloe's when Tom dumped me…"

"You'd give me a turn?" Delilah smiled and handed her the bowl. "No worries. You know you can crash here anytime. If I had a dollar for every time Chloe knocked on my door in the middle of the night, Simon and I could buy every ad agency in town."

"Honestly, I don't know how she survived all those back-to-back breakups."

"By stuffing her face and having a good pout. Since she was never very emotionally invested, she usually bounced back pretty quickly. God

forbid she and Ian break up. She'll be inconsolable."

"Like that'll ever happen," Larissa muttered.
"To either of you." It was clear both her friends
had found lasting love.

"True, but if it did, I imagine she'd be as messed
up as you are. Forgive me for saying this, but
you're more upset over this Carlos than you were
when you and Tom broke it off. Granted, you're
not crying the way you did then."

"I think I'm too sad to cry. I feel more numb
than anything. Like someone stomped on my
heart." Was this how Carlos felt after losing
Mirabelle? Probably worse. No wonder he was
so afraid to put himself out there again.

Understanding the man's position did not make
her feel better. "What am I going to do?"

"I'm afraid there's not much you can do. You
can't make a man interested in you."

"That's just it," Larissa said. "He is interested.
I know he feels the same way I do, but he's too
scared to let himself feel anything. Oh, Lord, I
sound like one of those letters in an advice col-
umn, don't I? Desperate in Manhattan."

"Dramatics aside, are you sure this isn't a rebound thing or the atmosphere getting to you?"

"Of course I'm sure," she said, stabbing the brownie with her spoon. Best friend or not, Delilah's question annoyed her. "Look, I know you and Chloe think I'm some kind of romantic ninny, but what I felt when I was with Carlos.... I can't explain. It's like something inside me clicked into place."

And there'd been a hole inside her since the moment she walked away on the beach. "It wouldn't matter if he was in Mexico, Manhattan or Mars. I don't feel whole without him."

She looked up at her friend. "Is it possible to find your soul mate only to have him not want you?"

"That's not really how soul mates work."

"That's what I was afraid you'd say." Appetite gone, she set the sundae aside. It was going to take a lot more than brownies and ice cream to make her feel full again. "So what am I going to do? And please don't say, give myself time, because I'll scream."

"Okay, I won't. I will, however, tell you to give *him* time."

"Excuse me."

Delilah reached across her to take the sundae off the end table. "Do you remember when I first fell in love with Simon? How he insisted he and I couldn't be together?"

Larissa remembered. A terrible trauma in Simon's past had him believing he wasn't good enough to be with Delilah.

"Well, my mother passed along some advice. She told me that if Simon was really my soul mate, he'd find his way to me. And he did. Took a while, but he did. If you remember, same thing happened with Chloe and Ian."

"But you and Simon worked together. You might not have been in a relationship, but you still saw him every day. And even Chloe and Ian were in the same city. Carlos is in Mexico, for crying out loud. What am I supposed to do, take the wedding coordinator job?" The idea crossed her mind more than once. That's how crazy she was about the man; she would relocate to the other end of the continent to be with him.

"Why don't we wait a couple weeks before trying something so extreme?" Delilah suggested.

"You think I'm being dramatic again."

"No, I think you're truly in love, and it stinks. Those weeks Simon and I were apart were some of the worst weeks of my life. You have to have faith that he'll miss you as much as you miss him, and that the loneliness will motivate him to do something."

Terrific. Her happiness rested on Carlos's ability to cope with loneliness. Larissa had a feeling she'd be waiting forever.

Wasn't heartburn supposed to clear up after a few days? It'd been almost three weeks, and the horrendous burning ache behind his breastbone hadn't eased up one bit. He shook out a handful of antacid tablets. Surely there was a limit to how many of these a person should take, as well.

"Those won't help, *primo*." Jorge walked into his office without knocking, an annoying habit that seemed to have increased over the past two weeks. "Antacid doesn't cure stupidity."

"I need it to survive your bad jokes," Carlos groused.

"No offense, but are you sure you're surviving?"

Carlos tossed back the tablets with a wince. Other than the heartburn, and a few bouts of insomnia, he was surviving perfectly fine. Business was doing well, the last of Maria's mistakes had been rectified, and every time he closed his eyes he saw Larissa walking out the door. What could be wrong? He pinched his brow. "Did you want something?"

"A letter arrived today that you should read. And before you ask, no, it is not from New York."

"What makes you think I was going to ask?" He knew better. When Larissa walked out the door, she walked out for good. He knew from the very start he wouldn't hear from her again.

The return address indicated the letter was from somewhere in Colorado. Carlos didn't recognize where. Upon opening, he found a gold-and-white note card. Nothing fancy. The hotel received dozens of similar cards every year. For some reason, however, this particular card made his stomach tighten. Slowly, he opened it and read:

Dear Señor Chavez:

I wanted to take this time to thank you for the incredible recommitment ceremony you and Señorita Boyd arranged for us. Linda didn't stop smiling the entire day and must have said a hundred times that it was better than she imagined. It truly was the trip of a lifetime.

Unfortunately, Linda suffered complications shortly after we returned. She passed away last week. Whenever I start to miss her, I pull out the photographs from that day. Seeing her smile, and remembering how happy she was helps ease the pain. Thank you for helping us make one last memory.

Sincerely,

Paul Stevas

PS: Could you please tell Señorita Boyd again how much Linda and I appreciated all her help? I don't have her address. Thank you.

The card slipped from Carlos's fingers. Poor Paul. Life kicked the poor lovesick bastard in the teeth exactly as Carlos knew it would. All that love and what happened? The kid was stuck at home with nothing more than memories.

Proof what he'd told Larissa was right.

Jorge picked up the card. "I remember this couple. They seemed like nice people."

"They were." Too nice for something like this to happen. "Have Louisa send flowers with our condolences."

"Are you going to let Larissa know?"

He nearly missed the question. It was the sound of Larissa's name that pulled him from his thoughts.

"The card says they don't have her address," Jorge said. "She'd probably want to know what happened."

She would be heartbroken, as well. Paul and Linda had become special to her. "Will you call her?" he asked his cousin.

"Don't you think she'd rather hear the news from you?"

He couldn't. Memories of her visit plagued him enough without hearing her voice.

Funny how Paul's memories brought him comfort, while thinking of a weeklong affair brought him nothing but insomnia and heartburn.

The ache in his chest started to spread. So much for antacid. "Given how we said goodbye, I'm sure hearing from me would be awkward."

"Since when has 'awkward' ever bothered you? I've heard you talk to guests over some pretty sensitive subjects."

"I never slept with any of those guests." *Slept with.* Sounded way too crude a term for what he and Larissa shared. When he was with her, he felt…

He felt.

Heaving a sigh, he shoved the thought from his brain, where it joined the countless other thoughts waging war in the center of his chest.

"She doesn't want to hear from me, Jorge," he said. Looking to the papers on his desk, he made a production of fishing through them. Perhaps his cousin would get the hint that he didn't want to have this conversation any longer.

No such luck. "I think she does, *primo*. I think she wants to hear from you quite badly."

"She also wants more than I can give her," Carlos snapped. "My calling would only open the wound. I'm asking you to do it. Now, if there's nothing else, I have work to do." He went back to shuffling through his paperwork.

Jorge stood, but rather than leave, he crossed around to the other side of the desk. Carlos tried to ignore him, but his hulking presence cast too big a shadow.

"What are you afraid of, *primo?*"

"Other than not signing off on these contracts in time?"

"You know what I mean. Larissa. I watched you when she was here. She was special."

More than special. "I'm not afraid of anything. Larissa and I had a weeklong affair that ended badly. I wish it hadn't, but it did. Life goes on." Eventually his guilt and regret would fade away. That's what this ache in his chest was, right? Guilt over leading her on?

"Rich talk, coming from you."

"What does that mean?"

"It means, dear cousin, that Mirabelle is dead."

"I know that," Carlos snapped. Dear God, but he knew that. Why were they talking about Mirabelle all of a sudden anyway?

"Because Larissa isn't," Jorge said when he asked. "She's alive and waiting for your phone call."

"No, she's alive and in New York City," Carlos replied. Even if he did call her, what good would talking do? Eventually she'd hang up, and he'd be faced with her absence again. "Calling her won't bring her back."

"Are you sure?"

"She has a life there. A family. A career."

"So?"

"So, she's not coming back," he said, slamming his hand on the top of his desk. Jorge's questions served nothing other than to churn up the acid in his stomach. Needing space, he shoved himself to his feet.

Outside his office window, the beach reached out to meet the crystal-blue water. It was a view he'd tried to avoid all month long. Too many associations.

"How do you know? Have you asked her?"

Of course he didn't ask her. "You saw how we ended things." Her asking him questions he didn't have answers to.

Not true. You know the answers.

Carlos closed his eyes. The voice had been taunting him more and more over the past three weeks, as well. Pushing him to have unwanted thoughts, asking him to open doors he'd be better off keeping closed.

"You know, I don't think I've ever hated her as much as I do right now," he heard his cousin say.

"Hate who?" Although he already knew the answer. Certainly couldn't be Larissa. She'd done nothing wrong. Nothing at all.

"I know it's wrong for me to say because she had so many demons. She needed so much. Too much. I saw how much you loved her."

"She was my world. Not that it did any good."

"I know, and that's why I hate her. Because she was too sick to see that and because when she died, she passed on her demons to you. I hate that she turned you into a coward."

Carlos shook his head. "I don't know what

you're talking about." He didn't want to talk about Mirabelle. Lately, when he thought of his late wife, the thoughts morphed into memories of Larissa. Her laugh, her innocent sense of wonder. He pictured her eyes when she saw the *cenote* for the first time, and her face every time their bodies joined together. Each and every memory twisted in his gut, begging for him not to push them away.

Perhaps Jorge was right. He was a coward. But couldn't his cousin see, cowardice was the only thing keeping his heart from ripping into pieces a second time?

Hasn't it torn already? The truth finally won the battle. All his lying to himself, all the walls he so desperately tried to keep erected, and in the end, Larissa still claimed his heart. Somewhere between the moment she opened her hotel door and their fight on the beach, despite all his best defenses, he'd fallen in love with her.

Whoever said the truth would set you free, lied. His pain was worse than ever.

"Call her, *primo*," Jorge urged.

"I can't."

Can't or won't? Larissa's final question came floating back, mocking him. So desperate to hear him admit his feelings. "She isn't coming back."

"How do you know unless you ask her?"

Before Carlos could argue otherwise, the two-way radio on Jorge's waist went off. A problem in the ballroom. "You better go," Carlos told him.

"Sending me off on an errand won't change my opinion, you know."

"Go."

"Fine, I'm going, but we will revisit this conversation. Along with the fact that we need a new wedding coordinator so I don't have to deal with catering crises every five minutes."

His cousin faced failure on both points. Carlos was done talking about Larissa. And as for a wedding coordinator, he doubted any future candidates would ever be as good as the woman who checked out a few weeks ago.

No one in general would be as good as her.

How long he stayed staring out the window, he didn't know. As he watched the sun drift from one corner of his window to another, hundreds of thoughts raced through his mind, all coming back to one central question. *What are you afraid of?*

Turned out his fear had been a self-fulfilling one, didn't it? With all his effort to hold Larissa at arm's length, to keep from feeling pain, he created even more.

Slowly, he walked back to his desk, where Paul Stevas's letter lay. What was it Larissa said that day on the beach? About Paul and Linda facing the bad together? He wished he could remember her exact words, but he'd been too busy scrambling to protect himself and they didn't permeate his brain until now.

Before he realized what he was doing, he'd taken out a piece of hotel stationery and started writing.

Dear Paul,
I am so sorry to hear about Linda. She seemed like a very wonderful person. It was obvious the two of you loved each other very much. I'm glad we could help you enjoy your final days together.

*Cherish the memories. Love is too precious
a gift to forget.*

He folded the note and set it aside to accompany
the condolence flowers. Love was a precious gift,
he thought. Mirabelle's demons hadn't let her see
that. And as a result, his demons hadn't let him
see the same thing when Larissa came into his
life. If only he'd been brave enough to realize
how lucky he was to be given a second chance
at happiness.

How do you know until you ask her?

He reached for the phone.

CHAPTER ELEVEN

Two weeks, five days and twenty-seven hours. That's how long it had been since she said goodbye to Carlos and flown back to New York, and the hole in Larissa's heart loomed larger than ever.

"If you love him set him free," she muttered. What a joke. She heaved her pen across her desk where it hit the postcard pinned to her wall before landing on a stack of media contracts. A nice red dot now marred the sky over the La Joya swimming pool. She should take the darn pictures down anyway. Looking at them only made the longing worse.

God, but she missed Carlos. Why did she have to be so stubborn about insisting he admit his feelings? She should have stayed the extra day and had one last wonderful memory. Granted, she'd still be sitting here in New York without him, but at least she wouldn't keep picturing the way his forlorn expression reflected in the glass as she walked out of the lobby.

No, you could torture yourself with some other memory.

"We brought you back a sandwich." Chloe rattled a white paper sack as she and Delilah invaded her cubicle doorway. "Roast beef with slaw."

"Thanks, I'll eat it later." Ignoring the look between exchanged between her friends, she set the back on the corner of her desk.

"You should have joined us," Chloe said. "Feels like summer has finally kicked in out there. It's even warm enough for you."

"Sorry I missed it, but I had too much work."

"Interesting how that's been happening a lot lately," Delilah remarked. "Work keeping you from lunch, that is."

"I don't see what's so interesting about it. No different from the way you work late all the time." Actually, it was a lot different and all three of them knew it. Her work might be piling up, but it was because she'd been unable to focus.

While her body sat in New York, her mind and heart were back in Mexico. The other day she went so far as to see if La Joya hired a wedding coordinator yet. At least if she were physically in Mexico, she'd feel like she was putting up a fight.

A hand settled on her shoulder. She looked up into Chloe's brown eyes. "It's going to be all right," her friend told her.

"Would you say that if this was Ian?"

Her friend's eyes widened a second, and she shook her head. "No."

"Exactly. It's not going to be all right as long as he's not part of my life." That's what she got for wanting real. Her life wasn't a life at all without him. She was no better than Carlos right now, existing in a void.

"You know what? I'm going back." Time she took a piece of her own advice. How could she expect Carlos to reach out and take a chance, if she wasn't willing to do the same?

She reached for the phone, only to have Delilah's hand curl around her wrist. "What will you do when you get there? Pick up where you left off?"

"Maybe."

"And then what?" Delilah asked. "Six months from now when he still won't open up to you, are you going to feel any better?"

"I don't know." She certainly couldn't feel any worse.

In the end, her phone rang, ending the argument. "Hi, Larissa, it's Jenny from first-floor reception. Can you come down for a moment?"

"Sure. I'll be right there." She hung up with a frown. "That's odd. First-floor reception wants me."

"Maybe someoné sent you a present," Chloe teased.

A present indeed. She and Delilah had been doing everything under the sun to cheer her up. They'd probably ordered a balloon bouquet or something equally silly. Forget what she said about not being able to feel worse. As horrible as she felt right now, she'd be completely lost without these two.

"I'd better go find out."

After four years of working at CMT, Larissa had come to expect all sorts of sights in their corporate lobby. None of them prepared her for the man standing at the reception desk.

Her heart leaped to her throat. "C-Carlos?" She whispered the name in case she was dreaming.

Carlos turned around and smiled. The shyness nearly broke her. *"Buenos dias."*

"Buenas tardes," she corrected. "It's afternoon."

"I guess I've got my time zones mixed up."

As he started toward the elevator, everything else in the lobby faded away. The only thing worth looking at was his face. Habit already ingrained, Larissa looked to his eyes. They shone like two dark jewels, bright and open. So incredibly, wonderfully open that she wanted to cry.

"Querida, no…" He cradled her cheeks in his palm, smoothed her trembling lip with his thumb.

"I can't believe you're really here," she whispered.

"I can't believe it myself, but I needed to tell you something, and face-to-face was the only way."

"Tell me something?" She felt her heart skip with a hope she dared not acknowledge.

Carlos nodded. "I wanted to tell you that you were special. That's the reason I did everything I did. Because you were…are…special."

He pressed a kiss to her forehead. To feel his lips after all this time… Larissa had to squeeze her eyes tight to steel herself against the thrill building inside. "I spent so many years thinking I was dead inside," he whispered. "Then this beautiful drunk blonde opened a door and I found out I wasn't dead after all. I was waiting for her. Only I was too scared to take a chance. Too afraid of how badly it would hurt when she walked away. So I tried to lock her out.

"Except," he said, smiling down with shining eyes, "she got in anyway. I've tried to deny the feelings for three weeks, but I miss you, Larissa. There's been a hole in my chest since you left."

Oh Lord, how she'd longed to hear those words. "There's been a hole in my chest, too. I've missed you so much."

"Same here, *querida.*"

It felt like an eternity, but at last, Carlos swept her into his arms. His kiss was honest and real, the connection instant. Gone was the distance she used to sense. Larissa wrapped her arms around his neck and kissed him back with an intensity that left them both breathless. When they finally broke, and she remembered where they were, she started to giggle.

"What's so funny?" he asked.

"Nothing." Looked like his kisses did have the same impact while standing on Madison Avenue.

Still, kisses weren't everything, and while she would far rather spend the next twenty four hours wrapped in Carlos's arms, they needed to talk. "So where do we go from here?" she asked, putting some distance between them.

"What do you mean?"

It meant dealing with nitty-gritty reality. Carlos coming to New York was a start, but if they were to make a real go of things, they needed to negotiate life beyond La Joya's romantic facade.

"For starters, we live three thousand miles apart. I have a job here. Delilah and Chloe are here." That she had been about to fly back to Mexico was beside the point. That was when she was depressed and thinking illogically.

"I'm well aware of the distance, and I've got a solution."

"Already? You've only been here five minutes."

"I've had a long time to think before I got here, and I realize I've been a selfish bastard."

"No—"

He held up his hand. "No, *querida,* I have been for a long time. By shutting myself off from the world. And, just because I've woken up, doesn't mean I have the right to ask you to give up your life. Not yet."

Larissa's heart started pounding. "Carlos, what are you trying to say?" She knew what it sounded like, but…would he really make that kind of commitment?

"I've put a call in to Kent Hotels regarding a position here in New York."

Oh my God, he was making that kind of commitment. "You're leaving La Joya?"

"The hospitality industry has always been a little nomadic. I've moved from hotel to hotel before. What's another move?"

"But it's your family's business."

"It's a business. Businesses can be replaced. Hearts can't."

"Wow." She didn't know what do say. He was willing to leave his family's business and move to New York City for her when neither of them knew what the future had in store. An incredibly gigantic chance for a man who feared getting hurt. That Carlos would take such a leap of faith *for her*... "I'm so humbled," she murmured.

"You're so worth it," Carlos replied.

If Larissa's heart ever had any doubt whether she belonged with him, those four words erased it. There was still one more question to ask, though. "And when things get rough?" She needed to know.

"We'll deal with them together."

"Are you sure? Because I want it all. The good, the bad and the ugly."

"So do I, *querida*."

They were both tired of keeping space between them. When Carlos stepped close again, Larissa melted into him. "I love you," she said, resting her head against his chest. "I don't care if it's too soon to say the words, but I—"

"Shh…" He pressed a finger to her lips. "Say them all you want, *querida*. I love you, too."

His kiss showed her just how much.

"Now," he said, planting one last kiss on the tip of her nose. "Why don't you take me upstairs to meet these best friends of yours? Then tonight, after you finish work, you can show me around my new adopted home."

"Okay, but I've got a better idea. How about I introduce you to Chloe and Delilah, and then, I show you how much I missed you."

He smiled. "I like your idea better."

"What can I say? I'm a terrific event planner." As she led him to meet the two most important women in her life, Larissa thought of how lucky she was. She'd gone to paradise to lick her wounds over lost love and discovered a love that was even better. What's more, with Carlos in her life, it wouldn't matter if she ever travelled to paradise again. Because paradise was wherever the two of them were together.

One year later…

"Tell me again why we came on this trip?" Simon Cartwright lifted himself from the infinity pool.

Water dripped from his Olympic-fit body as he walked to the nearby lounge chair to grab a towel.

"Near as I can tell," Ian Black replied, "it's so we have someone to talk to while our wives ignore us."

He smirked at the nearby table, only to have one of the women stick her tongue out in return. "Watch it, Mister. I'm not your wife yet," Chloe Abrams said, waggling her index finger at him. "I still have twenty-four hours to change my mind."

"Idle threats, Curlilocks. You and I both know you're stuck with me for life."

Rolling her eyes, the brunette turned back to the other women at her table. "I hate when he's right."

"You think he's bad now, wait until the two of you decide to have children," Delilah told her. "Simon's been strutting around like a peacock ever since the ultrasound. You'd think I was giving birth to the king of England." She squealed as Simon splashed water in her direction.

From her seat at the far end of the table, Larissa watched the whole exchange with misty eyes. She missed this—spending time with her friends. It'd been nine months since she returned to Mexico. True to his word, Carlos did stay in New York, although he took a year's leave of absence rather than find a new position. While Larissa knew beyond a shadow of a doubt the two of them belonged together, she told him they should take things slow, and he agreed.

New York lasted exactly six weeks. Surprisingly, it was Larissa who initiated the move back to Mexico. The decision came while she and Carlos were sitting in Bryant Park one brutally hot Sunday afternoon. If she was going to endure oppressive heat, she told him, she wanted egrets to sing her good-night. They returned to La Joya two weeks later. She didn't regret the decision for a moment.

Fishing the pen from behind her ear, she flipped open the file folder on the table in front of her. "Before Simon tosses Delilah into the pool, I want to make sure you're absolutely okay with the plans for tomorrow's ceremony. Are you sure you don't have any changes?"

"Other than the size of my bridesmaid dress?"

Delilah quipped. "It appears the future king has decided to take up residence in my rear end."

"No worries," Larissa told her. "The dresses I picked out are very figure-forgiving. You're not the only one whose rear end has decided to expand."

"Perhaps because someone feels the need to sample every wedding cake that comes through the hotel."

Carlos came strolling out from the restaurant, resplendent as always in his manager's suit. Twelve months together, and the way he moved still sent shivers down her spine. He smiled at her, his eyes warm and bright. "I guarantee tomorrow's ceremony will be flawless. After all, you're using the finest wedding planner in all of Mexico."

"She's also the only wedding planner who didn't have a wedding of her own," Delilah noted. "Noontime at City Hall? Seriously, what kind of wedding is that?"

Her cheeks growing warm, Larissa reached up and entwined her fingers with the hand resting on her shoulder. She and Carlos got married right before their return. "I had everything that mattered."

"And so do I," Chloe said. "I've got the man of my dreams and my best friends. Tomorrow will be the icing on the cake as far as I'm concerned." She giggled. "Sorry, La-Roo, did saying the word *cake* made your butt get bigger?"

"It did Delilah's," Simon said with a laugh. Before the brunette could retort, he gathered her in his arms and gave her a kiss. "And I love every inch."

"You better," she grumbled, kissing his nose.

"Ah, the sparkling cider is here."

At Carlos's announcement, a waitperson appeared bearing a tray with six glasses. "I thought we should have a toast to start the weekend," he said.

"To the bride and groom," Simon said, once the glasses were in hand.

"And good friends," Ian added.

Chloe leaned over and gave him a kiss. "To family," she corrected.

"No, to soul mates," Delilah said.

Larissa looked at the people around the table.

The six of them had endured a lot to find one another and now had nothing but lifetimes of happiness ahead of them. Who knew, when she walked into CMT Advertising four years ago, that a corporate orientation would bring her such enduring happiness? As far as she was concerned, the six of them shared one thing worth toasting above everything.

"To love," she said raising her glass. "To love."

* * * * *

MILLS & BOON®
Large Print – February 2015

AN HEIRESS FOR HIS EMPIRE
Lucy Monroe

HIS FOR A PRICE
Caitlin Crews

COMMANDED BY THE SHEIKH
Kate Hewitt

THE VALQUEZ BRIDE
Melanie Milburne

THE UNCOMPROMISING ITALIAN
Cathy Williams

PRINCE HAFIZ'S ONLY VICE
Susanna Carr

A DEAL BEFORE THE ALTAR
Rachael Thomas

THE BILLIONAIRE IN DISGUISE
Soraya Lane

THE UNEXPECTED HONEYMOON
Barbara Wallace

A PRINCESS BY CHRISTMAS
Jennifer Faye

HIS RELUCTANT CINDERELLA
Jessica Gilmore

0115 Rom LP

MILLS & BOON®
Large Print – March 2015

A VIRGIN FOR HIS PRIZE
Lucy Monroe

THE VALQUEZ SEDUCTION
Melanie Milburne

PROTECTING THE DESERT PRINCESS
Carol Marinelli

ONE NIGHT WITH MORELLI
Kim Lawrence

TO DEFY A SHEIKH
Maisey Yates

THE RUSSIAN'S ACQUISITION
Dani Collins

THE TRUE KING OF DAHAAR
Tara Pammi

THE TWELVE DATES OF CHRISTMAS
Susan Meier

AT THE CHATEAU FOR CHRISTMAS
Rebecca Winters

A VERY SPECIAL HOLIDAY GIFT
Barbara Hannay

A NEW YEAR MARRIAGE PROPOSAL
Kate Hardy

MILLS & BOON®

Why shop at millsandboon.co.uk?

Each year, thousands of romance readers find their perfect read at millsandboon.co.uk. That's because we're passionate about bringing you the very best romantic fiction. Here are some of the advantages of shopping at www.millsandboon.co.uk:

* **Get new books first**—you'll be able to buy your favourite books one month before they hit the shops

* **Get exclusive discounts**—you'll also be able to buy our specially created monthly collections, with up to 50% off the RRP

* **Find your favourite authors**—latest news, interviews and new releases for all your favourite authors and series on our website, plus ideas for what to try next

* **Join in**—once you've bought your favourite books, don't forget to register with us to rate, review and join in the discussions

Visit **www.millsandboon.co.uk**
for all this and more today!